ALONG FOR THE RIDE

Elaine Grant

I0536705

Table of Contents

PROLOGUE

THE HEAT FROM A TON OF animal sinew and hide rose beneath Seth Morgan's thighs as he hovered over the cramped bull chute. The dust of the rodeo arena filled his nostrils. The roar of a thousand eager fans in the stands echoed off the stadium walls.

Rotten.

He'd drawn a bull named Rotten for the final go-round. And from all he'd heard, the name fit.

Seth braced himself on the rails, waiting for the cowboy hanging over the side to pull the rope tight around the animal's girth, and then he eased down onto the bull's broad hindquarters. This huge yellow bull, a descendant of the notorious Bodacious, was gaining a reputation for tossing riders, as well as having a tendency for vicious retaliation afterward.

For a lot of riders, drawing Rotten was their worst nightmare. To Seth, he was just another bull that needed riding, and nobody had managed to do that—yet. An eight-second dance with this partner could score more than ninety points. Enough to give Seth the win today and ramp up his earnings to third, or maybe second place, in the overall standings. Yeah, he was ready for this ride!

Seth wrapped the rope taut around his gloved hand, then shifted forward, rope hand tight against his crotch. He popped in his mouthpiece, clamped his teeth hard and nodded to the gatekeepers.

The gate swung wide. With a wild snort and bellow, Rotten exploded into the arena, jackhammering his front feet into the ground with bone-jarring jolts. Bull snot flew in wide arcs as the animal launched into another gyrating buck, then whipped into a spin to the right. *Perfect,* Seth thought. *Piece of cake.* What he loved best in the world, this unbridled exhilaration.

One second...two...three... This bull was turning out to be easy. Why could nobody ride him?

Four... Stupid question. When Seth didn't fly off his back in those first few seconds, Rotten changed tactics. Rocketing off the ground, he whirled in the opposite direction, throwing Seth off balance. Known as an "eliminator," Rotten hated to lose as much as the cowboy on his back did. Smart, strong and unpredictable, the animal gauged his opponent and acted accordingly.

Seth slipped farther to the side. Only a split second to respond or land, as the announcers often quipped, like a "yard dart" on the hard arena dirt. Clenching the rope so fiercely it hurt, Seth released his leg grip long enough to shift back to center. *Chin down, shoulder in, focus on the withers. Anticipate!*

Five... Rotten ducked hard, jerking Seth forward toward the bull's head. One whack from those massive horns could be fatal. Unlike some of the younger cowboys, Seth rode without a helmet. His daddy and brothers would laugh him out of the arena if he came out of the chute wearing anything but his Resistol on his head. But a look at that swinging horn a foot away made him think again. *Too late now.*

Six... Seth pushed his fist hard against the rope around his riding hand to stay upright, away from the horns. Sweat soaked his shirt under the protective vest. Fighting to keep his free hand up to avoid any disqualifying contact with the bull, he forced himself erect.

Seven... Which apparently infuriated Rotten. The monster twisted like a corkscrew, throwing those massive horns at Seth. A contortion brought the wide head around so that one wild, red eye met Seth's with a chilling defiance.

Rotten plunged forward again. Seth felt his hand slip on the sticky rope. *No way!* One second to go. Sometimes you had to let loose and ride. Go for broke. Let your body and mind do what it did best. Seth shook off the stiffness of apprehension and spurred hard in rhythm with the bull's gyrations. The crowd went wild. If his teeth hadn't been clenched around his mouthpiece, Seth would have grinned.

Eight! The buzzer sounded. Seth had covered all three of his bulls for the event, earning a qualified score each time. He would move to first place on the leaderboard with this ride. Another event title, another buckle and a lot more money.

Elated, he reached to snatch the loose end of the rope and free his hand.

But Rotten wasn't finished. The bull plunged to his knees with a bellow. Now, when Seth needed it free, his glove stuck to the rosined rope. The animal rolled. With another hard yank, Seth freed his hand. But not in time.

A horn caught the side of his face. He heard the crunch of bone against bone, tasted blood mixed with arena dirt. He threw his arms up as if he could stop the steamroller mashing him into the arena floor, cracking ribs, crushing his left leg...suffocating him.

Then, as if the sun had been momentarily eclipsed, Seth saw daylight again. And heard noise. And felt horrific pain. His instincts told him to get up, run. But, helpless on the ground, his leg bent at a grotesque angle, his body wouldn't obey. Four massive black hooves shook the ground around his head.

He couldn't breathe. Rotten whirled, lowered his huge horns and lunged toward him. Seth braced for the worst.

Then a bullfighter threw himself in front of the animal. "Rotten. Rotten! Here!" he yelled.

He grabbed Rotten by the horns and swung the bull's head, shifting his momentum. Another bullfighter threw himself on top of Seth, risking his own life to save him. By the time the bull took off for the catch pen, the sports-medicine crew had surrounded Seth, holding him still, asking him questions he couldn't answer. Then everything went black....

CHAPTER ONE

WHAT NOW?

"Good morning, Kristin."

Claire Ford greeted the high school secretary and signed the visitors' register. Claire and the guidance counselor Betty Haynes had held their weekly meeting yesterday to discuss the upcoming summer ranch camp for troubled kids, but she'd gotten a call early this morning to come in at ten. Micah must have gotten in trouble—again.

"Go right in," Kristin said. "Miss Haynes is expecting you."

Claire's stomach churned. One more strike and Micah was not only out of her camp, but out of chances—at least at Little Lobo High School. Of the two boys and two girls registered in the summer camp, Micah Abbott, a tough seventeen-year-old only one strike away from reform school, was the kid who would benefit most.

She thought back to the preadmission interview she'd held with Micah and his mother—Micah's sullenness and his mother's assurances he would not only attend camp, but also do the mandatory follow-up assignments. Since then, Micah had been in trouble again, and now if he wanted to stay in school he had to finish the camp.

The counselor's door was open a few inches and Claire could hear the sound of conversation. She recognized the voice of Barry Nestor and smiled. The assistant principal, he had agreed to work for Claire over the summer as camp leader.

It was only days before her dream would be realized, the goal she'd struggled toward for several long years achieved. Finally she'd be able to try to help these kids get their lives back on track.

She tapped on the frosted glass of the door before opening it wide. Betty Haynes sat behind her desk, a venerable teacher and advisor with a reputation for dishing out fair but firm discipline. Dressed in a prim navy-blue suit, she had pulled her silver hair into a bun. The students

1

loved her, with the exception of those like Micah who spent far too much time in her office.

Barry was dressed more casually, in khaki pants and a light blue knit shirt. Heavy, dark-framed glasses gave him a bookish air that had the odd effect of softening his angular features.

Both looked glum, and Claire braced herself. "What's Micah done?" she asked, taking the seat Betty indicated.

The advisor made a wry face. "He and some others got drunk last night and decided to set off cherry bombs in rural mailboxes. They made the mistake of returning to gloat over their handiwork, and somebody got the license number off the truck."

Way to go, Micah. "I hope this won't interfere with his coming to the camp. I'm sure Barry and I can help him," Claire said. She saw the look the other two exchanged and didn't like it. "What?"

Barry cleared his throat, obviously uncomfortable.

"What?" Claire repeated.

"I don't quite know how to tell you this..." He hesitated. "So I'm just going to say it. I'm not going to be able to work for you this summer."

"You're...you're kidding, right?" She shifted in her seat, leaning toward him. "Barry, camp starts in a little over a week! We have to move the horses to the ranch and get the bunkhouse ready. And—"

"Listen, I'm sorry about this, but I got a job offer last night that I couldn't refuse. I'll be joining a group of psychologists in Phoenix. I've been trying to land a position like this for years. It's in my field of study, pays triple what I make here and, frankly, I'd be a fool to pass it up."

"But you made a commitment to these kids. They need you. *I* need you."

Barry lifted his hands in a hopeless gesture. "I'm sorry, Claire. I'll try to help you find a replacement, but I fly to Phoenix at the end of the week, as soon as school's out."

"I can't believe this. What about Micah?"

"I wish I could help you. I really do." Barry used a finger to push his glasses higher on the bridge of his nose. "I can't afford to turn down this offer. If I can't start right away, they'll find someone else."

Fighting back panic, Claire moaned. "This can't be happening." Where would she find a replacement for Barry?

"Claire," Betty said, "I have great respect for what you're doing with your camp. But, this is Micah's 'third strike' and the principal intends to expel him."

"Summer break starts next week. And Micah will be coming to camp the following weekend," Claire pleaded. "Just this once, couldn't you ask for leniency?"

Betty smiled sadly. "I am sorry. I was hoping Micah would stay out of trouble until summer. But I'm afraid with this last incident, and without Barry there..."

"In other words, you think I can't handle Micah," Claire said with a frown. "It's not fair to punish him because of Barry's decision."

"I know you're very capable, but Micah needs a strong male presence. Even if I could convince the principal to make an exception, I can't support his participation at this point, especially since we have another boy attending."

"We'll be on the ranch, surrounded by men. My father, Jon Rider—both are excellent role models. We'll be fine."

Betty propped her fingertips together and shook her head. "I'm sorry, Claire. They're not camp employees and will have other things to worry about. If you can't find a suitable replacement for Barry by early next week, I'll have to recommend that neither of the boys attend the camp."

Claire had dealt with Betty before and knew that the guidance counselor wielded enough influence to keep the students away from camp. Determined that Micah was not going to slip between the cracks, Claire stood, clenching her fists at her sides and forcing herself to remain calm. "Barry, I hope the job works out." Then to Betty, she said, "I'll find somebody. Please convince the principal to give him one more chance. I intend to have Micah Abbott at camp."

• • • •

STARING OUT THE WINDOW during math class, Micah saw Claire Ford leave the school building. Nosy bitch. No doubt she'd been talking to Miss Haynes. And no doubt when class was over he'd get a summons to the guidance counselor's office because Claire'd been meddling in his business again.

Like his life was *any* of Miss Haynes's concern. Or Claire Ford's concern, or anybody else's, for that matter. They all wanted to horn in where they had no business.

Wanted to fix him.

Well, he couldn't be fixed. His dad was in jail, his mother was a junkie who didn't particularly care what he did, and they lived in a crappy trailer on the wrong side of Little Lobo—hard to do, given the size of this Podunk Montana town. His parents were trash, his life was trash. He was trash.

Micah watched Claire detour to the playground where the elementary students were at recess. Miss Morgan, the third-grade teacher, met her at the fence that enclosed the play area, and they began to talk. Claire *was* hot, with a great butt—must be from riding horses all the time. If he thought there was any chance of tapping that, he'd be happy to play camp. But that jerk Nestor was going to be a counselor. Micah figured he might as well be in prison like his dad as go to that camp.

Micah's attention wandered to the front row of the classroom where Annie Whitman took notes on the lecture, her blond hair falling in silky waves over her shoulders. He'd heard she'd made it with every player on the football team.

She denied it, of course. But everybody knew it was true.

As if she could feel him staring, she turned her head and met his gaze. He winked. She straightened and jerked her head back around.

She hadn't lost her high-and-mighty attitude, that was for sure. Micah pressed his lips together. *Just wait, babe. You'll change your mind yet.*

An announcement crackled over the classroom intercom. "Micah Abbott, please come to Miss Haynes's office after class."

Micah rolled his eyes and stuffed his math book into his bag as the bell rang.

Right on time.

CHAPTER TWO

SETH YAWNED and opened his eyes to narrow slits. Midmorning light filtered into the room around fluttering curtains. He breathed in the smell of sweet grass and fresh air wafting through the partially open window.

Still sleepy, he closed his eyes again, drifting aimlessly in murky half dreams to a bright, sunny day more than three months ago. Victory within reach. A rank bull named Rotten. Riding on top of the world—then plummeting into oblivion.

Fighting the sensation of falling, Seth jerked violently awake. He wrenched upward, triggering a shaft of pain in his left hip and leg, which were held together with a rod and screws. He let out a yelp and collapsed onto the bed, snatching fast, shallow breaths, squeezing his eyes shut until the pain began to ebb. Meanwhile, he pulled a pillow over his head and tried to shut out the awful memory.

When he could breathe normally again, he shoved the pillow aside and looked toward the nightstand, which was lined with medicine bottles. The clock there showed it was almost 11:00 a.m. Another day in hell. He hated how the pain meds fogged his brain, but some days they were the only way to get a few hours of relief from the constant ache. Then there were the torturous workouts at the gym. They seemed to be doing next to nothing to restore strength to his thigh.

Almost three months after surgery he was still a cripple. He'd been able to put his full weight on his leg for a week now, but without crutches, he still struggled to keep his balance.

Seth sat up again, more gingerly this time. Slowly he shifted his legs over the side of the bed. He pushed himself to his feet, then stood still for a minute to let the pain ease before hobbling to the bathroom. After a hot shower that loosened him up a little, he poked around the kitchen, then nuked a large chunk of leftover casserole and sat down at the table with the steaming food and a glass of milk.

He hated to impose on his sister for so long, but the choice had been Libby's house or his parents' ranch. In truth, he'd rather be alone all day than have to deal with his father after the way they'd parted when Seth left home after high school. Seth's jaw tightened at the thought that once again he'd disappointed the man, even though he'd made a name for himself on the bull riding circuit. Rookie of the Year right out of high school, he'd earned a good living, been to the Professional Bull Riders World Finals in Vegas the last three years in a row, came in third last season. Damn it. He would have qualified this year, too. The way he'd ridden in the first few events, he could have ended up number one.

Then he could have returned home on his own terms to mend the rift between him and his father. Not now...not after that night in the hospital room when his father had assumed he was asleep.

"I knew he would end up this way. I tried to tell him," he'd heard his father say to his mother. "What's he going to do now that he's all busted up?"

Judd Morgan had no idea that Seth had heard, but the old resentment had flared up again and Seth would rather have gone to hell than drag himself home in disgrace.

Instead, he'd ended up here. Laid up at his sister's house, too dispirited to even follow the rest of the season on TV. He needed to get back on the circuit to bring in some money. He was losing his savings at an alarming pace, on expenses his meager medical insurance wouldn't pay. No company wanted to insure a bull rider, at least not at a reasonable rate, so he'd taken the minimum coverage. Even though he knew the bull riding mantra—it's not *if* you get hurt, it's *when* and *how bad*—he'd never intended to use that insurance. The best intentions...

Plus, he had a hefty truck payment, and insisted on paying room and board to his sister. Libby didn't want him to, but she didn't make much teaching, and he refused to mooch off her. His sponsors had been patient so far, but the nasty rumors that he'd never ride again were getting around, and those sponsors wouldn't wait for him forever.

Bile rose in Seth's throat as he recalled the orthopedic surgeon's dire prognosis after hours of intensive surgery.

"I'm optimistic you'll be able to walk without a limp again, in time." *Walk again? Of course, he'd walk again!*

"Cut to the chase, Dr. Tandy. When can I get back on a bull?"

"Bull riding? No."

Bull riding, yes! It was all Seth knew. All he loved. "I've got to ride, Doc."

"Is it worth the risk? You could do permanent damage."

If it wasn't worth the risk, I never would have climbed on the back of a bull the first time.

"Come on, Doc," Seth had countered, refusing to accept his fate. "Guys ride after breaking a leg. No big deal."

"The bone twisted apart in three separate places. If you injure it again…" He'd shaken his head and turned away from the hospital bed, writing on his chart. "Do yourself a favor, Seth. Find another career."

Seth made himself stop thinking about that. He grabbed his gear bag, went out to his truck and headed to the gym.

• • • •

T HAT EVENING, Libby brought home food from the local café. Seth didn't say so, but the fried fish, coleslaw and beans were a welcome change from the casserole he'd eaten for three days straight now.

"How did your workout go?" she asked.

Her sincere interest made him feel guilty. Her eyes searched his face and she shook her head, making her short blond hair bounce. "Not so well, huh?"

"I didn't go today." He wouldn't admit that he had driven all the way to Bozeman, only to take in a movie and drive home again.

"Seth, you can't do that! You have to be consistent with your rehab or you're never going to make progress."

"So what? Doc Tandy says I'll never ride again, anyway."

"Maybe not, but you'll do something else, and you'll want to be healed."

Libby must have seen despair on his face, because she changed to that firm older-sister voice she always used when he was hurt.

"It's going to take a while. There's no overnight fix and you have to have patience. Grab a couple of plates, okay? I'm starving."

Seth limped to the cabinet, laying napkins and utensils on the table, as well. "Patience," he griped. "You sound like Doc. If I hear that word one more time, I'm going to blow. And patience for what, if I can't ride?"

Libby began to eat, her face set in a worried frown. Maybe, Seth thought, he needed to move out, get away from his sister so she wouldn't feel so...burdened, and he wouldn't feel so guilty. The problem was, he'd sublet his apartment in Billings for the summer—a decision he now regretted.

"You're not going to ride bulls again," Libby said at last, "and you might as well accept it."

"I don't accept it!" Seth retorted. "And I don't intend to."

Libby put down her fork. "You know, changing your attitude might help a little."

"My attitude will change when I see progress."

The two of them ate in silence for a while. When Libby took her empty plate to the counter, she said, "Well, you can't just lie around this house all summer. You'll only get more depressed and down on yourself."

Seth followed her to the sink, where she began to wash the dishes. "Are you kicking me out?" he asked.

She handed him a plate to dry. "You know I'd never do that. But I want you to do me a big favor. I want you to help out a friend of mine this summer."

"Doing what?" Seth asked skeptically. He leaned against the counter, shifting his weight off his sore leg while he dried. "You know I can't work on a ranch with this useless leg and that's about all I know how to do. Besides, I have enough saved up to get by until I can ride again. If you need more rent I can pay it."

"Certainly not. You're welcome to stay here for free for as long as you want to—you're the one who insists on paying room and board." Libby finished the dishes and pulled the plug, letting the water flow down the drain. "I just hate to see you so low. If you had some sort of job, I think you'd feel better, and Claire is in a real bind."

"I'll feel better when I can ride a bull again." Seth dried the last glass and set it in the cabinet. He handed the dish towel to Libby and she spread it across the double sink divider to dry.

"You're being stubborn."

"As always." He managed a grin. "What's the deal with your friend?"

"Claire's the nicest person—and really pretty."

Seth straightened and gave his sister a warning look. "Do *not* try to play matchmaker."

She jammed her hands on her hips. "I'm not playing matchmaker. Claire just happens to be pretty, and she really needs help. She has a camp for at-risk youth starting next week at the Rider ranch, and the guy she'd hired to be in charge of the boys quit today. If she doesn't have a full-time male counselor in place by early next week, they can't come to camp."

"Stop right there. I'm not babysitting a bunch of rotten kids all summer."

"This isn't babysitting. These teenagers need help, and Claire's willing to provide it. She's worked for three years to get a camp started and has finally succeeded. Then Barry—he's the assistant principal at school, who was going to help her this summer—he got a great job offer out of the blue, a position that starts immediately. He quit on her today and she's afraid she'll never find a replacement in time."

"Nice guy." Seth shrugged a shoulder. "But I don't have the experience."

"No, but you're good with kids. And you could use something to occupy your time this summer."

"I'm good with *little* kids—and teenage girls," he said.

"Seth!"

He grinned again. "You know what I mean. Signing autographs and paying them a little attention, that's all."

Libby sighed in exasperation. "Anyway, Claire is concerned about one boy in particular. Micah Abbott. He's been in a lot of trouble this year. If he can't attend Claire's camp, accomplish the work there, he won't be allowed back in school next year."

"So what's the problem with this Micah? Sounds like he needs more than a slap on the back and an autograph. And that's about my limit."

"I don't know much about him other than he has a bad home life. Claire's camp is his last hope."

Seth had never minded assisting somebody in need—changing a flat tire or lending a buddy a few bucks. But spending his summer herding a bunch of teenagers was a bigger commitment than he was willing to make. "Libby, I wish I could help your friend out, but I don't think I fit the bill for what she needs."

"Would you at least go talk to Claire? Maybe you could just fill in for a few days to give her time to find somebody permanent."

"I'll think about it, okay?"

"Okay, but don't think too long. She needs help fast." Libby's voice held a rare edge of irritation. "And you *could* do this one favor for me. After all, I did you one, letting you come here, instead of making you go home to the ranch. I probably should have anyway, so you and Dad could make up. He wants to, you know."

"No, I don't know that," Seth said. "He's never done anything to make me believe it."

"And when have you given him the chance? You won't even talk to him. Even in the hospital you didn't want him in your room."

"Why would I? I did exactly what he always said I would. Ended up with my face in the dirt and busted up. I didn't want him rubbing that in."

"None of them would have done that. Everybody was worried to death about you."

"Yeah, well, Dad had a funny way of showing it."

"What do you mean by that?"

Seth shrugged. "Just something I heard him say in the hospital."

"What?"

"I don't want to talk about him anymore. I'll think about helping your friend." Seth felt trapped between the frustration of having an injury that prevented him from doing what he wanted to do, and the guilt of refusing his sister after all she'd done for him. He'd always hated being beholden, even to his family. "I'm going to bed. 'Night."

He gave Libby a peck on the cheek, then hobbled to his room to watch TV and sulk behind closed doors. He slumped into a chair in front of the TV and used his cell phone to call some of his buddies. He wanted to catch up on the latest standings, see if his name had already dropped off the list of forty-five top-ranked riders, but nobody answered.

Were they checking their caller ID and deciding not to talk to him? He hoped not but had to admit his attitude hadn't been great lately. He couldn't travel, and the others had to, or else they made no money. His travel partner, Jess Marvin, had been forced to pick up another buddy to defray expenses, but usually touched base every few days.

Sometimes Seth imagined that he saw wariness in the eyes of friends who visited him, as if what he had might be catching and if they hung around him too much, some of his bad luck might rub off and they could be the next one laid up. A lot of rodeo riders, like many athletes, had an unhealthy dose of superstition. Wearing a lucky hat or chaps. Dropping to a knee on the arena floor to give thanks to God after a ride or a save.

Who needed negativity when you had to go out and ride the next day? So his buddies had gone on with their lives and left Seth behind.

He picked up the Pro Bull Riders schedule from the floor beside his chair and studied it. No wonder they didn't answer. They were riding tonight and the rest of the weekend, right up the road in Billings. He could drive there tomorrow. Limp around, breathe in the intoxicating scents of livestock, sweat, and food from the concession stands. Take in the heady noise of the arena: the screams of the girls in the stands, the excited snort and grunt of a bull eager to get that rider off his back and that flank rope loose, the yells of the other cowboys urging their comrades on...The shouts of the bull riders luring a rampaging animal away from a fallen rider.

Seth remembered that sound well enough. And the pain, and the mortification of knowing he had to be hauled out of a hushed arena on a gurney. Yeah, he could drive up to Billings for all that. Sure.

He sailed the schedule into a corner, where it hit the wall and slid to the floor. No way in hell.

No, he'd just stay here with Libby all weekend and help her weed her flower beds. He might be doing that the rest of his life the way things were going.

CHAPTER THREE

"**WONDERFUL!** You're doing great. Cluck to her to keep her moving."

Claire watched as fifteen-year-old Rachel Rider, one of her young volunteers, led a Shetland pony around the dirt paddock behind the Little Lobo Veterinary Clinic. Rachel's twelve-year-old sister, Wendy, worked as a side-walker, her hand resting on the leg of a tiny helmeted girl sitting in a saddle that was too big for her, even though it was the smallest available. On the other side of the horse, another Rider girl, thirteen-year-old Sam, served as the second side-walker.

Another sister, eleven-year-old Michele, also volunteered for Claire's therapeutic riding program. Claire certainly appreciated Jon and Kaycee Rider's dependable girls. Without them, she feared she would be begging for volunteers to keep her program going in the tiny community. The family's generosity was overwhelming. Kaycee let Claire use the stables and paddocks behind her veterinary clinic and Jon had donated a bunkhouse on his ranch for her summer camp.

With her petite frame, nine-year-old Natalie Hughes could have passed for a five-year-old. Thick glasses made her blue eyes look huge. A combination of neurological and physical problems had stunted her growth and robbed her of the freedom of movement normal in children her age. Yet in the months since she had become one of Claire's pupils, the child had improved dramatically and now could sit unaided in the saddle. Soon Claire planned to give her the reins to learn to guide the pony, although one of the volunteers would have a halter rope to maintain control, and side-walkers would be in place on either side of her at all times. Still, given Natalie's limited abilities, it would be a major step forward.

"Now, lift your hands over your head," Claire told her. "That's good. The girls won't let you fall."

Natalie's body moved loosely with the pony's easy sway. She was game, and never hesitated to attempt whatever exercise Claire asked of her. She held her hands overhead for a minute, then let them drop.

"Great job," Claire said. "Now, say 'Whoa, Sheffield.'"

"Whoa, Sheffield," Natalie repeated.

The pony obediently stopped near the gate, waiting for Rachel to lead him through. Once in the covered cross-tie area outside the stables, Claire lifted the child down, hugging her for a long moment before settling her into the electric wheelchair on the concrete pad where her mother waited. Claire tried not to question God why kids like Natalie and the others she saw daily in her therapeutic riding program had been afflicted with such dreadful conditions, but their indomitable spirits always amazed her.

"Bye, Claire," Natalie said, turning her wheelchair on a dime and heading for the family van, where a lift would place her inside, wheelchair and all.

Her mother smiled at Claire. "Thanks...for everything. She's so much more confident now and happier all around. It's wonderful."

"I think she'll continue to improve as she gets stronger," Claire said. "She's almost ready to hold the reins. Maybe in a couple more lessons."

"Oh, she'll love that. See you next time."

Minutes later, the van pulled out of the parking lot, and Claire left the pony in the care of Rachel and Sam, so she could catch up on her administrative work. Claire's office and the tack room were located down a breezeway connecting the paddock area to the back row of stalls. Three stalls on the inside ell of the stable looked out onto the covered work area, and she had use of five more stalls along the outside perimeter. A nice wash rack was located behind the stables and the covered area was big enough to cross-tie two horses and still leave room for her challenged riders to maneuver.

Before her next lesson Claire had time to update her charts and continue her search for somebody to replace Barry, so she settled behind her desk to get busy.

A few minutes later she heard another vehicle pull into the parking lot, but she didn't bother looking up. As well as people coming and going at the vet clinic, there was a constant influx of customers for the Little Lobo Eatery and Daily Grind next door, not to mention the bed-and-breakfast behind the café.

The sound of approaching footsteps caught her attention, especially the uneven gait. She put aside her paperwork and went to the door. The man crossing the stable yard walked with a decided limp, favoring his left leg. When he looked up and found her watching him, his face registered surprise and embarrassment.

"Hello. Is there something I can do for you?" she asked.

"I'm looking for Claire Ford." The deep, confident voice belied his obvious discomfiture. A black Resistol hat sat low on his forehead, and a crisp, starched shirt and creased jeans complemented a lean, strong frame.

"You've found her," she said with a smile. "Are you here to set up therapy?"

He glanced down self-consciously, then lifted his eyes to hers. "Well, ma'am, I probably need a little, but that's not why I'm here."

"Oh, sorry," Claire said. "I shouldn't have assumed."

He offered a slight smile that brought a dimple to his left cheek. "I'm Seth Morgan, Libby's brother. Libby wanted me to stop by about some camp." He crossed his arms. "Doubt I'm what you're looking for, but I told her I'd come as a favor, and here I am."

"Seth, nice to meet you." Claire reached out a hand and they shook briefly. So this was Seth Morgan. That explained the limp. Libby had told Claire about her brother's injury. What she'd failed to mention was the attitude. Bull rider. Rodeo cowboy. What else should Claire expect? But this cowboy wouldn't be riding bulls anytime soon. "Thanks for coming by. Libby told me you might be interested in working for me this summer."

"It's more like Libby wants me to find something to do. I owe her big-time but asking me to play wrangler to a bunch of kids is a bit much."

Too bad he hadn't knocked that chip off his shoulder when he fell. Claire noticed him favoring his hurt leg. "Come into my office and let's talk."

Since yesterday, she'd made a dozen phone calls, with no luck. At this late date, anybody who might have the summer free had already found employment. Unfortunately, Claire hadn't interviewed anyone for the job beforehand, since Barry had been the perfect candidate—or so it had seemed. Lesson learned. Always have a plan B.

Seth followed her inside and eased down into a chair, his relief obvious as he removed his hat and laid it in his lap. He was a good-looking guy in his mid-twenties, around Claire's age. Light brown hair showed traces of fading sun streaks, and that athletic physique hadn't come from a gym.

"Like I said, I doubt I'm what you're looking for." His brow furrowed. "I've never done anything like counseling before."

Claire toyed with a pen on her desk. "Right now I might gladly take any male over twenty-five." She realized how that must sound to a stranger, and when he chuckled, the heat of a blush crept up her neck.

"Well, I fit that bill. Looks like we're both in a bind."

Boy, did he ever fit the bill—in spades. Golden eyes the color of a cougar's held her gaze and turned up the thermostat under her skin until she forced herself to break contact and try to concentrate on what the job entailed.

"Look," she said. "I'm desperate to find an authority figure for one of the boys."

"Micah? Libby told me a little about him."

"Yes, Micah Abbott. The guidance counselor won't allow him or the other boy to attend if I don't have a man as a full-time assistant camp director."

"Assistant camp director? You're getting way out of my league now."

"Won't be too difficult. I need a male authority figure to help keep Micah in line, that's all."

"And you think just having me around will do that, when the entire school system can't? Won't take a smart kid long to test a banged-up cowboy." Seth's gruff voice carried a hint of frustration, maybe even anger.

"Even if you were whole, I would expect you to avoid physical force."

"Number one, I *am* whole, lady, just broke my leg," Seth snapped, pushing himself up from the chair and setting his hat back on his head with a thump. "And number two, I think you need to find somebody else to wrangle this kid."

If his attitude was a reflection of how he would handle students, she might just be creating more problems by hiring him. Besides, the sex appeal oozing from his pores might be too much of a distraction. Still, she had to have an assistant.

"I'm sorry, I should have said 'even if you were completely healed.'" Claire rose also. "There are other ways of asserting authority besides being physical, you know."

"No, I wouldn't know much about that. I'm pretty used to physical."

"Libby told me you were a bull rider."

"Am. I *am* a bull rider," Seth said, his words clipped with irritation.

"I understood from your sister that you wouldn't be able to ride again after this injury."

The color drained from his face and his breathing quickened perceptibly. "Libby's got no business saying that. That's my decision to make."

"I must have misunderstood," Claire said quickly. "I thought she mentioned that was the doctor's prognosis."

"The surgeon is probably the best there is, but he's not God. I hope you find somebody for your camp." Seth spun toward the door, and in the process lost his balance. He caught hold of the door frame to steady himself.

Claire's first instinct was to rush to help him, but she refrained. He froze in the doorway as if paralyzed, and she realized he was in pain physically as well as emotionally. His pent-up frustration and fear were palpable.

Claire's nurturing instinct kicked in. "Seth," she called quietly. "I could really use you this summer. Libby almost promised you'd help me out."

He wouldn't turn back to her. "She's got no business saying that, either."

"I do need help." Claire eased around her desk. "If I can't give the guidance counselor a name by early next week, my camp may not be able to open."

Seth's grip on the door frame tightened until his knuckles went white. "You need somebody else," he said between gritted teeth. "Like you said, somebody whole."

"I wouldn't offer you the position if I didn't think you could handle it."

He didn't respond, but he didn't leave, either.

"And, Seth," she said, "I could work with you to strengthen your injured leg and improve your balance. That's what I do for a living, you know. Therapeutic riding. Think about it overnight, okay?"

He shook his head in a brusque, dismissive movement and started for his truck.

"I'll be here at eight tomorrow morning, if you change your mind," Claire called after him.

CHAPTER FOUR

"**SETH, GET UP.**"

Libby's voice outside his bedroom door startled him awake.

He groaned and muttered, "What?"

"Get up and go tell Claire you'll help her."

Seth sat up in bed, the covers pooling around his bare stomach. His sister had harangued him all last night for turning Claire down. "Don't start on that again, Libby."

"I just talked to her. She's at the stables for a few hours this morning. Get your butt dressed and get out there."

Seth did a double take, staring at the closed door. Libby never used an off-color word, not even *butt*. "Come on. I told you I don't want to—"

"This is the way it is, Seth! Either go work for Claire this summer or I'm going to tell Daddy you're just wallowing in self-pity, and that he should come up here and get you."

Seth breathed a few choice words that Libby couldn't hear. Just what he needed—his father and two of his older brothers on his case all summer. Lane, the one closest to his age, might cut him some slack, but his oldest brother, Howdy, wouldn't. Sometimes Howdy acted as if he thought he was Seth's father anyway. "Okay. All right. I'm getting up."

"Good. Get up and stay up." She was in full schoolmarm mode now and not to be denied. "I'm teaching early Sunday school today. If you get things straight with Claire in time, it wouldn't hurt you to come to church."

"Don't count on that," Seth muttered.

"What?" Libby said though the door.

"I said I'll try," he called. "You can stop the lecturing now. I'm up."

He heard Libby cross the hall to her bedroom and close her door.

It was 7:00 a.m. He hadn't been up this early since he'd gotten out of the hospital. Before his accident, he'd never lain in bed past six. Maybe it *was* time for him to get back to normal. But he hated the thought of facing Claire Ford again after yesterday. She must really be desperate if she was willing to hire him in his current physical condition.

He shook his head. He wasn't used to a woman studying him with that analytical, sympathetic expression, something akin to pity. Seth didn't want anybody, especially a good-looking woman, feeling sorry for him.

His jaw clenched as he recalled how other women had reacted to him, screaming his name and cheering while he flung his hat across the arena in celebration of a great ride. Pressing around after the event as he loaded his gear into his truck. Sidling up to him in the bars the cowboys frequented. Offering to come to his hotel room or inviting him to theirs. Depending on how pretty she was or how drunk he was, Seth had taken some of them up on their offers. They had never looked at him with pity.

His blood pumped hard with rising anger. He sure as hell didn't want Claire pitying him. He wanted that old sense of power, that cocksure attitude that had carried him to victory in and out of the arena. Sweat popped out on his forehead when he stood, and the ache in his leg threatened to lay him flat again. The anger turned into a hot, fluid rush of terror. What if he never got back to where he had been before the accident? What if it just never happened?

Stop it! He forced his breathing back to normal. Chased the dread out of his mind. No way would he surrender to a broken leg. He'd faced injury before and looked at death every time he settled on a bull's back. This was just a bigger setback than most. Still, as he hobbled to the shower, uncertainty gripped his stomach, like a hunger he couldn't sate.

A hot shower and a big dose of ibuprofen eased the pain. He rubbed a hand over his freshly shaved jaw and splashed on aftershave.

With a towel wrapped around his waist, he went to the closet in search of clothes. As usual, Libby had arranged his shirts by color and lined up a row of perfectly pressed jeans next to them. Maybe that was another reason she wanted him gone. Her life had been a lot simpler before he barged in. In all fairness, he had tried to convince her he could do his own laundry. He couldn't help it if she was such a mother hen.

He pulled out a pair of jeans, rummaged in his drawer for underwear and moved to the bed. One of these days, he'd be able to step into pants again like a normal human being. Since the surgery, he hadn't been able to lift his left leg high enough to dress standing up. Instead, he had to sit and drag the pants on like an old man. It had absolutely infuriated him at first, but he'd grown resigned over the weeks. Either do it that way or go naked—not an option as long as he lived in somebody else's house. At least he could put his boots on by himself now.

He went back to the closet for a shirt, which he put on and tucked in. His eye caught a glimpse of his best pair of chaps hung across a heavy-duty hanger at the far end of the closet. He fingered the long, silky silver fringe, which feathered across his hand like a woman's hair.

On a whim, he pulled the chaps off the hanger and buckled them on, along with his other riding gear. Standing before the mirror, Seth allowed his gaze to run the length of his reflection, from the black hat cocked on his head to the crisp white shirt and black flak vest emblazoned with sponsor emblems, to the long shimmering fringe on black-and-red leather chaps, and to square-toed, spurred boots that had seen more than one rodeo.

He lifted his eyes to stare at the oversize trophy buckle on his belt, the one for the win that was announced while he was en route to the hospital—his "Rotten buckle," as he called it. Seth's heart plummeted. The image in the mirror was the man he used to be. The man he still wanted to be. The man he might never be again.

A bull rider—all he'd ever wanted to be.

Seth snatched off the vest and chaps and threw them on the closet floor, followed by the trophy buckle. He found another, unassuming belt and took the spurs off his boots. He wasn't going around pretending to be something he wasn't, and right now he didn't know what he was.

He recalled Claire's offer to help him rehab his leg. Maybe that wouldn't be a bad idea. And Libby had him over a barrel. He'd do anything not to have to tangle with his dad right now. Maybe by the time summer was done, he would be healed enough to make a decision—one that might change him forever.

• • • •

MICAH SAT ON THE rickety front steps of his hotter'n hell trailer. Inside, his mother lay sprawled across her bed in a stupor, the result of cheap liquor and ill-gotten prescription drugs.

Knee-high weeds surrounded the trailer and the rusting pickup truck parked alongside. It had sat there since Pop went to prison. When his mother had said he couldn't drive it, Micah had taken it without permission. Until she'd thrown the keys somewhere out in the overgrown field, and he'd never been able to find them. What did it matter now? All the tires were flat, and the truck probably wouldn't start, anyway.

Micah propped his elbow on his knee and rested his chin in his palm. Stuck out here in the middle of nowhere, with nothing to do...His buddies wouldn't be by today. Most of them were grounded for a month of Sundays for getting drunk and blowing up mailboxes last week. It had been fun while it lasted. Especially driving back around and laughing at the angry owners.

Unfortunately, one of them had nailed the culprits. The boys would have to replace all the mailboxes with their own money and labor. The ones who had money would pay for the boxes, and the ones who didn't, like Micah, would have to do the grunt work of digging out the old posts, pouring fast-acting concrete, setting the posts, waiting for the concrete to harden, then attaching the new mailboxes. A lot of payback for a quick thrill.

Micah wasn't grounded. His mother didn't care if he blew up mailboxes. She didn't care what he did as long as she had a stash of booze and pills. He closed his eyes, feeling the hot sun burn his face.

At least he felt something, even if it was just physical. He'd long ago learned to zone out most of the emotional stuff. It had begun about the time his father lost his job with a big construction company, a good-paying job painting the walls of new buildings. When Micah was young, the family had enjoyed a decent life. They'd lived in a modest house in town, the truck had been new and shiny, and Micah was allowed to sit on his pop's lap and "drive" down the dirt roads outside of town. His mother had been pretty and kept a tidy house and cooked good food. Life had been okay until three years ago, when his father got caught stealing some paint from work to make the house look better...and worse, the investigation revealed that he'd been sneaking other material out the gate for years. Ten in the pen.

That was then, this is now. Micah shoved himself up from the porch, went down the steps to tinker with the rusted-out truck. If he could just get it going again, he'd be free....

• • • •

"**G**OOD MORNING."

Claire jumped at the sound of the deep voice. Her hand flew to her heart as she swiveled around in her chair. She'd been so lost in thought she hadn't heard Seth come into the barn. He lounged against the door frame of her tiny office, arms crossed, watching her.

"Sorry, didn't mean to scare you."

"I'm not scared," she said, her heart still double-timing. "Just startled. How long have you been there?"

"Long enough to know you concentrate very well—and if I can sneak up on you, just about anybody could."

Claire found herself mesmerized by the steady eyes that locked with hers and wouldn't let go. "That's not good," she said.

"Depends on who's sneaking, I guess." Seth pushed away from the frame with his shoulder and shoved his hands into his jeans pockets. "Well, I'm here to take that job offer, if it's still open. Libby's going to throw me to the wolves if I don't."

Claire smiled. *Any port in a storm, sometimes. Thanks, Libby.* "I hate for you to be pushed into something you don't want to do, but I *am* desperate."

"Like I said, I don't have much choice, either." He cleared his throat and added, "I was wondering about that therapeutic riding, too. Do you think it might heal my leg quicker?"

"We could sure give it a try."

"I guess that sort of thing's pretty expensive, though, and my insurance has paid all it's going to for physical therapy."

"Therapy lessons aren't cheap," Claire agreed. "Most of my students are subsidized by donations."

"That's what I figured," Seth said, shrugging. "It was a good thought, anyway."

In truth, she didn't recoup the cost of maintaining the stables and horses or upkeep of equipment, not to mention her modest salary, from what she charged her students. Most of her funding came from generous donations, most of her help from teenagers who volunteered their free time.

"How about this—you work at camp in exchange for therapy. However, I expect a firm commitment from you to stay the whole summer. I can't afford to lose you halfway through and have to send the boys home."

Seth didn't look happy, but he nodded. "Fine. It's not like I've got anything else waiting. I'm pretty much sidelined for the summer. So, what all does this camp involve?"

"Pull up a chair," Claire said. When they were settled, she began, "The camp starts next Sunday and will last four weeks. An old bunkhouse on the Rider ranch has been converted to a dorm, thanks to donations from Jon Rider and Cimarron Cole. Do you know them?"

Seth shook his head. "I haven't met many people since I've been here. Libby says I've been a hermit."

"Jon's wife, Kaycee, is the vet next door, and Cimarron and his wife, Sarah, own the café and bed-and-breakfast on the other side of the parking lot. Jon donated the bunkhouse on his ranch and Cimarron rebuilt it into a dorm."

"Sounds like you've got some good connections."

Claire laughed softly. "My dad, Clint, is Jon's foreman, and I helped Cimarron with his little boy, Wyatt, before he married Sarah. He's shown his gratitude by supporting both my camp and my therapeutic riding school."

"So how much does a riding lesson cost?" Seth asked.

"If I charged what it costs me to run the school, at least a hundred fifty bucks an hour."

Seth whistled softly. "That's steep."

"Yes, but who can afford that around here? Nobody. That's why the donations are so important. I charge from sixty to ninety dollars an hour depending on what the family can afford."

He raised an eyebrow. "I couldn't afford that for long. You must be planning on paying me a lot."

"No, sorry, not all that much. Barry was a volunteer, but I did plan to offer a small salary."

"Which I can exchange for a few therapy sessions?"

"Yes, we can do that."

"Deal," Seth said. "You've got an assistant camp director. So, what now?"

"Paperwork. Lots of paperwork." Claire pulled a folder from a desk drawer and handed it to him along with a pen. "There's an application and other forms inside. One concerns general medical information. I'll need your doctor's signature on a physical exam form—you'll need a physical if you haven't had one lately. I'll also need a recent therapist's evaluation before you start riding. I can fax the forms to speed things up."

"Sure. My surgeon is in Dallas and my therapist is in Bozeman." Seth gave her the names.

"Dallas? That's pretty far away for checkups, isn't it?"

"I use an imaging center in Bozeman to do X-rays and send them to the surgeon to evaluate. My therapist sends him reports, too, probably not much to his liking these days. I'll have to go back in a few months, but for now long distance works."

"I see," Claire said. She wrote down the names, then pointed to the packet of papers in front of him. "Also, there's a release to run a background check on you."

"Background check? In case I'm some kind of pervert?"

Claire leaned back in her chair and studied his face. He had the softest eyes, and a smile that quirked up endearingly on one side.

"Something I have to do on anybody I hire, since I work with children and teens. One of the local deputies runs the checks, and he usually gets back to me right away. But if there are any surprises that might show up, I'd appreciate you bowing out now. Having Micah come to camp is very important to me, and I don't have time to spare."

"No surprises. I had a speeding ticket two years ago, but I paid it. No bad credit—not yet, anyway. No arrests or anything like that. Not on any child-predator list, either."

"That's good to know," Claire said. She trusted that Libby would never have suggested her brother for the job if he had a questionable background, but she had to be sure, anyway, to safeguard her campers.

Seth opened the folder and flipped through the pages. "Whew, this could take a while."

"Part of the process. Lots of red tape. But if you have time to fill them out now, we could get some of the orientation out of the way today."

"What kind of orientation?"

"First, how to handle the horses."

He gave her an incredulous glare. "I know how to handle horses. I grew up on a ranch. I've been around livestock since I could walk."

"I don't doubt that, but my horses are trained for special-needs children and adults. They're accustomed to being treated the same way each time." Claire was used to this spiel. She had to give it to all new riders and their parents and caregivers. The youngsters were generally not a problem, but older students and adults tended to resist learning new techniques. She hoped Seth was flexible.

"You'd have to go through the orientation, anyway, if you want therapy. I have a license to maintain and insurance requirements to fulfill." Claire braced for his reaction, then added, "And you'll be required to wear a helmet when you ride."

A look of surprise and sheer defiance crossed his face. "A helmet? You're kidding."

"'Fraid not. It's a safety requirement for me to keep my insurance."

He looked away, frustration obvious in his eyes. She figured he was cursing her silently, but she had to stick to her guns.

"Lady, you must have a hell of an insurance company."

She waited for him to back out of the whole deal. A muscle in his jaw twitched as he stared down at the stack of papers.

"So, are you still with me?" she asked.

He glowered. "I don't go back on my word. But I might just forgo the therapy."

"That's up to you. I'll catch up on some computer work while you complete the forms." She turned to her monitor and finally he picked up the pen and began to fill in the blanks.

When he finished, about twenty minutes later, he closed the folder and pushed it toward her. "Can we go pet the horses now?"

Claire ignored the sarcasm. "Sure, come on. I'll let you have your pick, if you're good."

"Oh, I'm good, lady. I'm real good."

Claire shook her head and rolled her eyes. Seth gave her a crooked smile in return.

They walked slowly down the row of stalls. One after another, horses pressed friendly noses against the bars and were rewarded with a pat from Claire as she introduced them to Seth. A small bay quarter horse nickered as Claire stopped before her stall.

"This is Sweetie Pie. I've had her for about two years. She's a darling with the little kids. And this is Captain Jack."

In the next stall, a large Appaloosa with a black patch around his left eye stuck his nose through the bars as far as he could.

"As in Captain Jack Sparrow the pirate?" Seth said, rubbing his knuckles gently along the soft muzzle.

Claire laughed. "Actually, yes. His former owner loved that movie, but I can't bear to call him that. He's no pirate. In fact, he's a nice horse, but I'd want to start you on one with a smoother gait."

She sensed Seth's body stiffen and glanced at him. He was obviously biting back words. She pretended not to notice as she moved on to another stall, where an old buckskin stood munching hay from a wall rack. "Jiminy Cricket."

"Beg pardon?" Seth said.

"The horse. Jiminy Cricket. He's twenty-eight, and I pamper him by only putting very lightweight children on his back. He's a dear and deserves an easy old age."

Seth nodded. "I got no problem with that. We do that on the ranch, too."

"You have a ranch?"

"In northern Wyoming. My parents' ranch where I grew up."

"I should have remembered that. Libby's told me a couple of stories about her childhood. I hope you weren't the brother who operated on all her favorite dolls to heal them."

"Nope, that was Will. I was still a baby, so that's one thing I couldn't be blamed for. About the only thing, though. Besides, Libby got a whole bunch of new dolls out of it and Will had to work off the cost of them."

Claire laughed, as Libby had done when she told the tale, while admitting she'd been horrified when she discovered her dolls bandaged all over. Even worse was when she'd removed the bandages and found her dolls tattooed with permanent red marker to mimic surgical incisions.

"Will's a surgeon in New Orleans now," Seth said. "Guess he was just practicing for his future. My brother Cord's a lawyer in Denver and Howdy and Lane are still at the ranch helping Dad. I seem to be the only one..."

His voice trailed off. Claire waited for him to go on, but he didn't, so she resumed the tour of the stables.

They stopped again before a stall with a sleek palomino pony inside. The small animal whinnied and ambled to the door, his outstretched nose barely reaching the bars in the top half.

"I wouldn't recommend Sheffield, even though he is pretty. You'd end up carrying *him*, as tall as you are."

"I don't think that'll be a problem. I told you I'm not going to do that therapy."

"Because of a helmet? Come on."

Seth grew downright sulky, but again Claire ignored him. He definitely needed to lose the negativity, but instinct told her he was using it as a front to hide his real feelings.

"One more." She rounded the corner and opened a stall door. Inside, a big, plump piebald mare lifted her head to stare at Seth with mild interest. Her huge hooves were feathered at the fetlocks, and her white mane and tail looked stiff as wire. Her conformation indicated draft-horse blood.

"She'd be good for a crusade," Seth said, leaning against the stall post.

"Now, don't make fun of her," Claire said. "Her name's Belle and she's sweet as can be. If she's ridden five minutes or all day, she'll never complain. She's the only one other than Jack that I use for adults."

Claire brought Belle out on a halter, led her through the breezeway to the covered work area and hooked her in the cross ties. "I'm sure you know how to groom."

"Nah, why don't you show me?" When she held a currycomb out to him, he gave it a questioning frown. "Is this a test?"

"You might say so."

He cocked an eyebrow, but took the tool from her and began to loosen the dust and debris on the horse's coat with quick efficient strokes. His leg might be weak but muscles rippled under his shirt as he worked his way along the horse's back. Claire could see him visibly relax, and gradually the frown left his face. She was glad to hear him talking softly to Belle as he worked, and Belle flicked her ears back and forth, listening. He finished with a dandy brush from the toolbox, leaving the black-and-white mare shining. Claire cleaned the horse's hooves, then unsnapped the cross ties and handed Seth the rope.

"I'm going to teach you to lead now."

"You walk off and the horse follows," he said. While he didn't actually say "duh," his tone certainly implied it.

"Not around here," Claire said. "You stand beside her head and ask her to move forward with you."

"What?"

Claire took the lead rope and stood beside Belle, holding it several inches below the snap. She moved her hand forward without taking all the slack out of the rope. Belle stepped forward and they walked in a tight circle before Claire brought her back to Seth.

He heaved a sigh. "Lady, you're crazy. What's the difference?"

"Please stop calling me 'lady.' My name is Claire." She handed him the lead. "And there is a difference."

"Yeah, fine." Seth tugged on the rope, not hard, but with an air of impatience. Belle didn't budge.

"Don't yank," Claire said. "Just move your arm forward a bit. She'll respond. Like this."

His biceps tensed when Claire laid her hand on his long, scarred fingers. She felt the soft sprinkling of light hair on the top of his hand and the edges of calluses on the underside. Quickly, she moved his hand forward slightly until Belle took a step. Seth didn't budge and the lead rope grew taut. Unable to go forward, Belle crossed in front of them, the change in direction tugging Seth's arm around Claire's waist. He spoke softly in her ear, his warm breath causing her to gasp in surprise. "I have to say, this is a novel way to move a horse, but I like it."

He smelled good, of fresh soap and aftershave. Of a subtle maleness that quickened Claire's breath. The heat of his muscled forearm burned through her thin T-shirt and her skin prickled with an odd anticipation. He made no effort to turn her loose, and his breath feathered the tiny hairs along her neck. Her initial urge was to lean against that rock-solid chest and enjoy the moment, see what he would do next. Then Belle snorted and Claire caught herself. She pushed Seth's arm away.

"Let's see you do it on your own."

He narrowed his eyes, jutted out his jaw and said, "Aw, it's a lot more fun when you help. I work much better hands on."

Her chest heaved with embarrassment and an unwanted physical attraction, to boot. She couldn't afford to be taken in by this bull rider's charm, especially since he was her employee. She drew away from him to a more comfortable distance.

"We don't have all day."

With a wicked grin, Seth stepped to Belle's side and did as Claire asked. She gathered her wits and explained other specifics about the handling techniques the horses understood. He listened and learned.

When Claire noticed him favoring his leg more, she brought the session to an end. "That's enough for now. I have lessons this afternoon and some errands to run. We'll start again tomorrow morning at eight."

She glanced over her shoulder as she led Belle back to the stable. Seth walked slowly toward the parking lot, shaking his head. She wondered if hiring him was the right thing to do and thought he might be asking himself the same thing.

· · · ·

W HEN CLAIRE ARRIVED HOME that night, she found her father setting out plates on the kitchen table.

"You cooked?" she said, laying her messenger bag on the built-in desk in one corner of the kitchen.

Since enrolling at Montana State University as a freshman, she'd lived in the small foreman's house her dad occupied on the Rider ranch. As cramped as life was in the tiny two-bedroom house, she'd been glad to have her father back in her life after many years of separation. He was growing older now, and the sorrows of his past were etched on his face, yet he rarely asked about her mother and never mentioned her brother, Cody, at all. A couple of times, when they sat on the porch in the quiet evenings, she'd thought about bringing the subjects up, but never found the right opening.

"Humph," Clint said. "You know I don't cook unless I have to. Rosie promised to bring over beef stew in a few minutes."

Rosie, the Riders' live-in housekeeper, cooked, cleaned and kept the house in order as well as looking after seven kids ranging from the four girls who volunteered for Claire to a set of nine-year-old twins named Zach and Tyler, and Bo, a rambunctious five-year-old.

"She seems to cook for us a lot lately," Claire said, tweaking her dad's cheek to annoy him.

He pulled away with a frown. "Keeps you from having to do it when you get home. Seems like you'd appreciate it."

"Oh, I do," Claire agreed. "But it *is* getting more frequent."

"Wipe that matchmaking grin off your face, missy. Ain't nothing going on between me and Rosie."

Claire grinned wider. "Never said there was."

Clint set the last of the silverware in place and leaned a hip against the kitchen cabinet. Long, lean and lanky, her father was the quintessential cowboy, from his old, well-worn boots and jeans to his weathered face and the squint lines around his blue eyes. That applied to his outlook on life, too. No frills, no nonsense, no compromise. He had never been as hard on her as he'd been on Cody, but then, Claire had rarely seen him after her mother divorced him and took her to California. There her mother struggled to make a good life for them, building a successful career as a horse gentler. From her Claire had learned independence and the value of hard work, as well as her skill with animals.

"You ain't saying, but you're giving me that look," he drawled.

Before Claire could respond, Rosie yoo-hooed and came in through the back door, holding a cooking pot with insulated oven mitts. A large-boned woman with graying brown hair, she had a round, kind face that one would pick out of a catalog for the perfect grandmother, even though she was younger than Clint. The stew smelled delicious. The youngest Rider girl, Michele, followed with a shopping bag filled with containers of corn and green beans and a basket of hot bread.

"Rosie, you are too good to us," Claire said, helping set out the dinner. "Won't you stay and eat."

"Love to, but I can't. Kaycee and I are going to be up half the night sewing the girls' Scout badges on their sashes. I promise I will another time."

"We're holding you to it, right, Dad?" Claire winked at Clint, who turned red as a chili pepper under his tan. He mumbled something, and Rosie and Claire exchanged a conspiratorial look.

Michele skipped toward the door. "Gotta go. See you later."

"I've got to get back to the house, too," Rosie said, tucking the oven mitts into her apron pocket.

Clint followed her out the door, and Claire could hear their low voices just outside. She wondered what they were discussing. Her father rarely talked about anything of importance, mostly mundane day-to-day news. Never anything personal. She took her place at the table and waited for him to join her. Within moments, he returned, filled his plate and sat down, digging into his food.

"I hired a camp assistant today," Claire said.

Clint gave her a look from under bushy eyebrows. "Who?"

"He's the brother of a teacher I know, Libby Morgan."

"He's a counselor, like you need?"

Claire gave a soft laugh. "Not even close. I called everybody I know and nobody was available for the summer. Seth's a bull rider. He broke his leg earlier this year."

"Seth Morgan? I hated when I heard about that. I've seen him ride. He's damn good."

Oh, he's damn good, all right. Claire's body tightened at just the thought of his arm around her that morning and his warm breath on her face. She exhaled softly. She was going to have to break herself of that reaction, and quick. No way should she be responding to his male appeal at all, considering the circumstances.

"A *bad* break, according to his sister," she told her dad. "She says he won't be able to ride again."

"I bet that's not what he thinks."

"You're probably right. But from the way he limps, he may be in for a long haul back."

Clint paused with a forkful of food halfway to his mouth. "I'm surprised you hired him, knowing how strong you feel about rodeo and all."

"To be honest, Dad, I'd have taken anybody with a good recommendation at this point. I can't let Micah down."

"Yeah, I know, but what if Morgan up and quits on you when he finds out you don't like how those poor little rodeo bulls are treated? How will that affect your camp?"

"Now you're making fun of me. I can't see where my opinion would matter to Seth. Besides, he committed to the whole summer and you know a cowboy's word is everything." She smiled at her father, who had drilled that into her head from the time she was a baby. "Anyway, why would it even come up?"

"You'll be on the ranch. The first time you take one of the ranch hands—or Morgan—to task for the way they handle an animal, he'll figure it out. And if he gets released to ride early, I guarantee you he'll be gone before you can count eight seconds."

"I'm not even going to think about that. Libby says the doctor's not going to okay any bull riding. Seth wants to do some therapy riding, and I think the first time he straddles a horse he's going to realize he doesn't want to be on a bull—although he might back out of therapy before he gets started. I told him he'd have to wear a helmet."

"Now *that* I'd like to see," Clint said with a broad grin. "I surely would."

CHAPTER FIVE

SETH APPEARED at the stables right on time the next morning. One point for promptness, Claire thought. And another for looking flat-out sexy this morning in crisp jeans and a creamy shirt that accentuated his tawny eyes. With that black hat set low on his forehead, the cockiness she'd noticed yesterday was in full force, despite the unevenness of swagger.

"So, I'm here. What do I get to learn today? How to saddle the pony?"

The attitude nixed both those newly earned points.

Ignoring the sarcasm, Claire said, "I thought we'd start with therapy. I received the release from your doctor this morning for supervised sessions."

"Supervised! I told you I was going to skip that, anyway. I'll find a horse to ride somewhere else."

"Your decision, but Belle's saddled and ready. Wouldn't do any harm to see if a go-round helps."

She saw his hesitation, sensed that he really wanted to try but was embarrassed.

"This morning would be a good time," she added. "Things are quiet and there's nobody around."

"Except y—" He bit off the word.

"I'm not the problem," Claire said. When she held out a helmet, he rebelled completely, almost recoiling from it.

"I'm not wearing that damn thing."

"You will if you expect to ride."

"Come on. I've never worn a helmet in my life—for anything. And I don't need a lesson. I just want to get on the horse."

There. He'd admitted it. Claire wanted to smile. Just as she'd suspected, he did want to ride, probably more than she could imagine.

43

"Rules. Sorry." Claire lifted the helmet toward him and waited. Finally he set his cowboy hat on the bench, took the helmet and plopped it on his head. "Satisfied?"

"Buckle it."

She could feel his rising frustration, but he fastened the strap. Claire bit back a smile. He was as cute as anything with that helmet on, but she didn't dare say so.

He eyed the mare's back skeptically. "What kind of saddle is that?"

"It's specially made for my students. High cantle with extra support in the back, and the pommel is easy to hold on to. Lead her over here to the mounting block."

"Hell, I'm not going to do this. I didn't expect remedial riding lessons." He reached for the helmet buckle.

"Probably just as well," Claire said without missing a beat. "I doubt you can get on her at this point even with the mounting block."

"What?"

"You heard me. We should wait until you've healed more."

His lips pressed into an angry line and his chest heaved. "I can get on the dam—"

"You're going to have to stop that cursing before camp. Might as well be now."

"I can get on the horse," Seth said sharply.

"Do it, then."

She never would have been so blunt with one of her students, but Seth was a grown man and she figured he'd cowboy up and meet her dare.

· · · ·

Seth moved to the end of the ramp that led to a platform used for the more challenged riders. The first step up the incline shot a hot poker of pain through his thigh. If Claire hadn't been standing nearby, waiting for him to fail, he would have turned tail and gone home. Instead, he grasped the rail, set his jaw and somehow made his way to the top. Then came the next challenge—getting on the horse. To do so he had to balance on his left leg while he swung his right up and over the low saddle. Problem was, he couldn't bear full weight on that leg long enough.

"Don't try that," Claire said, as if reading his mind. "Face the horse and lean on her to support yourself, then swing your right leg over."

God, he hated this disability. Ordinarily, he'd be asking a girl like Claire for a date, hoping to score later in the night—from the first time he'd seen her, he'd been intrigued by the intelligence in her pretty face and the ready smile that put a sparkle in her gold-flecked hazel eyes. Instead, she was telling him what to do, and he was barely able to follow through. How had he come to this?

But Seth had never been one to back down from a challenge, even if this might be the most humiliating thing he'd ever done. He took Claire's advice and eased his leg over the horse's rump. As he settled into place on Belle's back, he thought he might have to do it all over again, because the pain that exploded through his hip and groin muscles almost knocked him to the ground. Anything other than this gentle, plodding horse would have put him in the dust in a lot less time than a bull ever had.

"Do you want me to lead her for a while?" Claire asked.

All Seth could do was shake his head. He held out one hand for the reins while he clutched a shock of mane in the other to stay on. Claire didn't look as if she wanted to, but she looped the knotted reins over Belle's head and gave them to him, her long, slender fingers lingering on his hand until he had a good grip.

"Okay, nudge her and she'll walk."

Right, nudge her. Every muscle in *both* thighs revolted when he pressed the horse's sides. Seth thought he might break a few teeth, he had to grit them so hard to keep from groaning aloud. Then Belle moved forward and the torture got worse. He'd never have believed he'd have to struggle so hard to stay in the center of a horse's back. After all, his dad had had him in the saddle from the time he could sit up as a baby!

Claire walked beside him in silence, her sun-streaked ponytail swinging with each step. If she laughed at him, he just might come apart. The helmet seemed to shrink a couple of sizes with the pressure growing in his head from angry frustration. His face beaded with sweat, and a rivulet trickled down the small of his back. Concentrating on breathing to combat the agony, he barely noticed where they were going. When he did look, he was surprised that he'd only gone halfway around the paddock.

"Do you want to cut across to go back?" Claire asked, concern evident in her voice.

Seth gave a curt shake of his head. By God, he'd make at least one round. Then he had to figure out how to get off without breaking his neck.

Half an hour later, Seth had a new appreciation for the ground. Sliding off Belle's broad back proved less challenging than getting on, but still hadn't been a cakewalk. He was forced to hold the rail going down the ramp because his legs were shaky and he couldn't tell which thigh hurt worse.

At the bottom, Claire gave him a broad smile.

"Hey, you did great!" she said.

The rage that flooded Seth took him by surprise. He despised condescension. He hadn't done great. He'd been like a wet noodle in a steam bath up there. He snatched the helmet from his head and all but threw it at her, then put on his hat.

"Like hell, I did great!" he snapped. He took Belle's reins and limped away to the stables, knowing Claire was watching his every step. At least she didn't come after him.

He unsaddled the horse and led her to her stall, closing himself inside with her.

This couldn't be his life.

He crossed his arms on Belle's broad back and laid his head down on them, waiting for the shaking to pass, breathing in the earthy, soothing horse scent rising from her warm skin. Belle nickered softly and nuzzled his hair, her breath tickling his ear. Seth lifted his head and stroked her wide face.

"What am I going to do if this is all that's left, Belle?"

CHAPTER SIX

MENTALLY, CLAIRE KICKED herself all the way to her office. She'd said exactly the wrong thing to Seth. Maybe her six-year-olds ate up that kind of praise, but he had issues that negated her well-intentioned encouragement. Her blunder went deeper than failing to give Seth encouragement in a meaningful way. Now she worried whether she'd be able to read her summer campers any better. The wrong word to one of them had the potential to set their progress back, when her goal was to move them forward.

So many people had helped her get a start, so many friends and relatives believed in her work. Sometimes the weight of the responsibility she'd taken on and the possibility of disappointing her supporters was intimidating.

She had plenty of work to do to before the group lesson this afternoon. The ticking of the big, round clock over her desk made her realize how quiet and peaceful the stables were.

A few moments later, Seth appeared in the doorway, his broad shoulders blocking the light coming into the room. He stood there awhile, then seemed to force the words out. "I took care of Belle."

"Good," Claire said. "Look, Seth, if we're going to be working together all summer, you need to get past this attitude. You're not the first bull rider who's been bucked off and hurt."

"Never said I was. And I wasn't bucked off. Everything happened after the ride."

"See? You get defensive over the least thing. That won't work with these kids I've got coming."

He glared at her. "So fire me."

"I don't want to fire you. I want you to come to terms with this injury and do it before my camp starts."

"You got any magic wand to make that happen?"

"Look, I know what you're going through is tough, but if you saw some of my riders you might think again. You're out of commission for a few months—for most of those kids, the disability lasts a lifetime. You'll see this afternoon, when Natalie and Ben come. It might put things in perspective."

Seth settled into a chair by the desk. "So how long have you been doing the handicapped riding thing?"

"*Therapeutic* riding," Claire corrected automatically.

He shrugged. "Okay, so how long have you been at it?"

"Full time? Over a year now."

"You have a degree in therapeutic riding?"

She smiled. "Not specifically. I have a B.S. from Montana State in exercise science, and I've done extensive training in therapeutic riding."

"I see."

"I've got a ways to go. I'd like to study physical therapy at some point, maybe get a degree. Did you rodeo in college? Get a degree in bull riding?" Her tone was teasing.

The light, however, went out of his eyes. "No. But maybe if I had, I'd have learned to stay on better."

Claire, figure it out. You can't kid around with this man. At all.

He made a wry face, then said, "Sorry, attitude again. So, if you're not going to fire me, what's next?"

Claire pulled a thick notebook from her bookshelf and laid it on the desk in front of him. "This is the camp manual," she said. "You need to familiarize yourself with it before camp begins. Feel free to ask questions. I'm also open to any ideas or suggestions you might have."

She placed a folder on top of the manual. "These are the files on the campers who are coming."

Seth glanced through the contents. "Four kids? That's all?"

"Yes. I'd like to expand in the future, but for now I only took students from the local high school. These were the four recommended by the counselor. Of course, Micah's been 'unrecommended' a number of times since."

"Why are you determined to have him?"

"He seems to need the most help. I'm afraid he might end up on the street if he doesn't go back to high school next year."

"In that case, let's hope you can get through to him."

"*We*. Let's hope *we* can get through to him."

"Right," Seth said, sounding a bit skeptical. "So what's the schedule for this camp?"

"It's a four-week in-residence camp on a ranch near here."

"Like a wilderness camp? Survival type stuff?"

"No. I would like to do that someday, but not this first year. There'll be hikes and trail rides, but my main goal is to give these kids a break where they're not under a lot of pressure. A safe haven, you might say. I want them to learn to trust one another and adults, to learn to rely on themselves and others. There'll be a lot of equine-assisted therapy. Each camper will be assigned a horse to care for. We'll have structured and unstructured time with the horses."

"The horses you have here? Belle and the rest?"

"No, the campers will have the use of well-broken ranch horses. However, you and I will move my horses to the ranch on Saturday, since I'll also be doing my lessons through July. You should plan to move into the bunkhouse on Saturday, too."

Seth thought for a moment, then said, "Do you mind if I bring my own horse?"

"There's plenty of room for another horse, of course, but...I guess I didn't realize you had a horse here to ride. And I'm concerned about your leg on an unreliable horse."

Seth grinned. "Trust me, he's as old and gentle as your Belle. Pretty red roan that my mother named Rhubarb, of all things. He's retired back home, but I can get one of my brothers to haul him to the ranch."

Claire was drawn to those unusual light eyes so intently fixed on her, and not for the first time decided he might be dangerous to her well-being. She'd discovered that the indentation in his left cheek when he smiled wasn't a dimple at all, merely a scar cut deep into his skin. And she suspected his nose had been broken. Both flaws gave character to an already ruggedly handsome face. An interesting face that made her heart beat in strange ways.

"Let's see how your leg adjusts to riding over the next few days, then make that decision. Now, before I have to get ready for my lesson, let's go over your duties and how the camp will run."

For the next couple of hours they worked together at Claire's desk as she detailed her expectations of him and the basic overview of the camp. They went through the manual section by section: first aid, camp policy and procedure, discipline, daily activities. The book included a layout of the ranch, detailed maps showing line shacks, mountain elevations, ravines and water sources.

"Impressive," he said when they closed the thick notebook at last. "You seem to have everything covered."

Claire smiled and said, "And yes, there *will* be a test."

"A test?" Seth glanced at her uneasily.

She laughed at his expression. "You don't like tests?"

"Not a lot. One reason I was glad to get out of high school. But I'll manage."

"I was joking. That's your copy of the manual. Feel free to take it home and study it. Even if there's no test, you need to know it backwards and forwards so the campers have no reason to question your authority."

He nodded. "Got it. What else?"

"I have lessons shortly, so nothing more today. I'd like you to stay and observe, however, because some of my teaching methods are going to apply to the campers, too, along with the interaction with horses, and team-spirit exercises. Then tomorrow we need to drive to Livingston to do some shopping."

"Shopping? For what?"

"Items for an incentive program for the teenagers."

"Incentive program?"

"They can earn rewards through chores and group participation. You'll see the point system and rules in the manual."

"Interesting," Seth said.

The sound of giggling interrupted them.

"Hi, Claire. Everybody's here for the lesson," a high-pitched voice called.

"Come on in," Claire invited. "These sisters are my wonderful volunteers."

Seth rose as four girls entered. Claire introduced Rachel, Sam, Wendy and Michele Rider.

Rachel and Sam stared at Seth as if moonstruck. Michele, always precocious, spoke up. "So you're going to be at our ranch all summer?"

"Looks like it," Seth stated.

"That's cool. You'll like it."

"I'm sure I will," he said politely.

"Let's get going, girls," Claire said, then turned to Seth. "Come watch the lesson."

· · · ·

ROUNDING THE CORNER of the stables Seth stopped short. He hadn't expected so many people. At a rodeo or bull riding event he knew how to work a crowd, but these were just regular people, not fans—and he was a little rusty on social skills.

"Come, meet everybody," Claire said, approaching the stable work area where two horses were secured in cross ties. She introduced him to two women who looked to be in their thirties—students' mothers, Claire told him.

Seth smiled and tipped his hat to them. "Ladies."

Sam Rider assisted a boy who wore leg braces and leaned on metal crutches as he worked diligently on Belle. A few feet away, a little girl in a wheelchair brushed Sheffield as far up as she could reach, her blue eyes huge behind thick glasses.

Claire introduced the pair as Ben and Natalie. As soon as she said Seth's name, Ben's eyes widened.

"Like the real Seth Morgan, the bull rider?"

Surprised, Seth said, "Yes, the real one. How do you know me?"

"I watch bull riding all the time when it's on TV. You're my favorite. When I see you ride, I pretend it's me. But my mom told me you got hurt. Can you still ride?"

Claire shot Seth a look he couldn't quite interpret.

"Not right now," he replied, trying to figure out what had upset her. "My leg's still healing."

"But you're going back, right?" Ben asked.

"You bet," he said. "As soon as I can."

Now Claire's eyes burned into his. What was it with her?

She looked mad as hell all of a sudden. Maybe she thought he'd skip out on her camp to go back to riding, but he didn't operate that way. She'd have to figure that out.

"Do you ride horses, too?" Natalie asked. She powered her chair across the space between them like a pro, the wheels bumping along the uneven ground. Seth realized after a moment of concern that she was securely harnessed into the chair and in no danger of falling out.

"Yes, I ride horses."

"Are you going to watch our lesson?"

"I thought I would."

Natalie grinned broadly.

"All right, all right, enough talk for now," Claire said. "Some of us have work to do." She began herding the children toward the stables.

"Natalie, Ben, around to the mounting block. Rachel, Sam, bring the horses."

Seth found a place where he could lean on the fence and see the action. The two mothers soon joined him. Again he touched his hat out of respect, as his dad had drilled into him. "Ladies."

At first the three stood in silence. Then Ben's mother said, "I can't believe my son got to meet you. You're one of his favorite riders. You've made his day."

Seth felt a twinge of the excitement of being recognized, but not in the same way as he used to, when he knew he'd be riding again. He gave a little nod and said, "I'm glad, ma'am."

The gate to the paddock opened, and Natalie and Ben, riding in tandem and accompanied by volunteers, drew everyone's attention. Claire moved to the center of the arena and the volunteers led the riders in a circle around her. Seth's gaze settled on Claire's lithe form and vibrant expression. Her straight brown hair, pulled into a ponytail, glinted in the sunshine. Jeans that hugged every curve of her hips and legs, along with a Western shirt molded to her torso, confirmed what he already knew—the woman had a fine body beneath those clothes. Seth blew out a controlled breath and shifted to rest his left foot on the lower rung of the fence.

Natalie peeked at him as she passed and gave a tiny wave, taking care not to lose her balance. Ben kept his eyes on his horse in total concentration. Seth knew that kind of focus. The boy didn't want to screw up in front of another guy, especially one he considered a hero. Both kids did remarkably well, in Seth's view, as Claire put them through a series of drills and games.

What a struggle those kids must have every day! At Natalie's age he'd been riding calves for the fun of it, and by the time he was Ben's size, he'd been his dad's best bronc buster. And he'd loved every wild minute.

Seth grew grim. Only recently did he have any idea how it felt to be crippled, and he realized he wasn't nearly as accepting and resilient as these kids seemed to be.

He felt a tug on his jeans leg and looked down to find four little boys staring up at him, each with a child-size white cowboy hat in hand. One of them held up his hat and a felt-tipped pen.

"My sister said you're Seth Morgan. Will you sign our hats?" he asked. The other boys huddled nearby, hats in hand, waiting anxiously for Seth's answer.

"Glad to, but let's wait until these kids are finished riding, all right?" he replied. "I want to see how they do."

"Sure. We'll wait for you at the stable."

When the lesson was over, the riders and volunteers headed out of the paddock. Ben's face broke into a broad grin when he saw Seth still standing at the fence, watching. The boy gave him an exuberant wave as he and Belle passed through the gate.

Back at the stable, the young boys crowded around Seth again, holding out their hats eagerly.

"What's your name?" Seth asked, taking the pen from one of what was obviously a set of twins. He turned the child's hat over to write on the underside of the brim.

"Zach Rider."

Seth read aloud as he wrote: "To my good buddy Zach." Then he whipped off his signature in the way that had become familiar to his fans, almost illegible but unmistakably his. The mark of Seth Morgan, bull rider.

Sidelined. Out of action.

He pushed the gloomy thoughts aside and took the hats one after another until he'd written something special on all of them. By then, Natalie's mother had powered down the side ramp of the minivan.

"Let's go, Nat!" she called. "Homework and dinner are waiting."

"Okay!" Natalie stopped for a moment in front of Seth. "Nice to meet you, Mr. Morgan."

"You, too. You're good riders. Both of you." Seth nodded at Ben, who was making his way slowly on his braces and crutches to the SUV where his own mother waited.

"Thanks," Ben said gruffly, but he seemed to swell with pride.

"Will you come back again?" Natalie asked.

Seth nodded. "I'll be around."

Claire had been right, Seth admitted silently. Watching Natalie and Ben humbled him. Whatever happened in his future, he'd get over the broken leg. These kids would never have that chance, short of some medical miracle. And yet he hadn't heard a single complaint the whole time. It was a lesson he intended to take to heart. And Ben's admission that he rode bulls vicariously through Seth bolstered his determination to return to the sport.

I'll ride again, Ben. Just give me a little time.

"A penny for your thoughts," Claire said, coming up to him after the vehicles had pulled away.

"Thinking about those kids and their dreams," Seth said. "Must be hard."

"It *is* hard. And I'd appreciate it if you wouldn't fill their heads with impossible things like bull riding."

Seth drew back in surprise at the fervor in her voice.

"I just answered the boy's question. Besides, what's wrong with him dreaming of bull riding?"

"He needs to learn to live with what he can do, not waste time on what he can't."

"I don't get that at all," Seth said. "Why discourage his dreams? What's left?"

"Reality, Seth. The reality of life."

He shook his head. "You take away the will to try if you take away dreams." He paused. "Anything else you need done today?"

"No, I think we're good. Be here early in the morning to head for Livingston."

CHAPTER SEVEN

SETH ARRIVED PROMPTLY the next morning for the shopping trip. He insisted they go in his truck, a late-model Silverado with all the options, including a five-CD changer loaded with an eclectic mix of music, from rock to country. At first they rode in silence, letting the music fill the cab.

After a few miles, Claire turned down the volume and began to discuss the particulars of camp. She was pleased to find that he had studied the manual closely overnight.

"Micah's going to be a handful," he said. "But it looks like he only started acting out when his dad was sent up."

"Acting out," Claire mused. "That's one way to put it."

"What I'm trying to say is that he might need no more than a strong father figure in his life right now."

"Well, that's your job. But I don't want you to think you can browbeat the kid into behaving. I want to help him, not set him back."

"Gee, thanks," Seth said dryly. "Just what I had in mind—beating the kid into submission. Anyway, I'm not quite old enough to be his father—I was thinking more like your dad, since we'll be at the ranch and—"

Claire cut him off. "No way. I told you I want you to help him. My dad's had his chance...."

He shot her a curious look. "What does that mean?"

She ignored him.

"No problem. I'll handle Micah," Seth eased the truck to a stop in front of Jenkins Farm Store. "Here we are."

Claire slid out of the truck, relieved to escape further questioning. Raz Jenkins, the owner of the old-fashioned general store, had offered merchandise as a donation to the camp. She exchanged pleasantries with him as he stood behind the counter, and they asked about each other's family.

"Glad you came to get your goods," Raz said. "Just tell me what you want and I'll bag it up."

"Thanks so much for your generosity," Claire said as Seth approached.

She was about to introduce the two when Raz said, "Well, I'll be. Seth Morgan! What are you doing in these parts?"

Seth shook Raz's hand. "I'm working as Claire's assistant camp director. You look familiar. How do I know you?"

"We met in Vegas. I was one of the judges at the PBR World Finals last year when you came in third. I was sure thinking you'd end up in first this year. Hated to hear you got hurt."

"Thanks," Seth said. "I do remember you now. Are you judging again this year?"

"Hope so. I'll know by the end of the summer. Any chance you'll be back by then?"

Claire listened with interest. Maybe she needed to do a Web search on this bull rider everybody seemed to know and find out what kind of rodeo star she had on her hands.

"I'm waiting on the doctor's release, maybe in late summer or early fall."

"But you *are* coming to the Livingston Roundup over the Fourth of July holiday, aren't you?" Raz pointed to a big poster on the wall behind the counter advertising the popular, long-running rodeo event, as well as the kickoff hoedown and parade.

"I just might. Good rodeo. I used to go every year I could." He turned to Claire. "That would be a great day trip for the campers."

"No."

"No? Just like that, no? Why not?"

"We'll talk about it later."

Claire looked over her list. "I need boots—two pair for boys and two for girls. And dress shirts for each camper. And hats. They'll need hats." She glanced at Seth's expensive Resistol and said, "Not quite *that* good a hat, though."

Seth rewarded her with a rare full smile and touched the brim of the hat. "I'd hope not," he said. "Because if you bought this hat, you have to get these." He picked up a pair of hand-tooled boots with a price tag that would bankrupt her camp.

"I don't think so," she said, guiding his hand to an inexpensive pair nearby. "This is more what I had in mind."

Before she could react, Seth turned his hand over and clasped hers firmly. "Works for me."

His gaze lingered on her face a long moment before he turned to the rack of boots, his eyes twinkling with mischief. Claire quickly pulled her hand away and gave him a slip of paper.

"The boy's sizes are listed here. Pick out a dress shirt for each of them, a belt and a couple pairs of socks. And hats more in accord with *these* boots."

"Yes, ma'am, whatever you say," he drawled, and made his way to the shirt racks.

Raz was looking far too curious, and Claire pushed her own list of items in front of him. "Can you fill this order while I pick out the girls' shirts, boots and belts?"

"No problem," he said, taking the paper.

She wondered what tidbits of gossip might start due to Seth's unexpected familiarity. He'd been joking, no doubt, but she cast a furtive glance at his broad back moving among the racks, wondering how many women he'd bedded, winning them over with little more than a warm hand and hard body. Which led her to wonder what being in bed with him might be like, which led her to blush—and again attract Raz's attention. This time the man grinned like the Cheshire cat. Claire hurried off to take care of business.

Raz bagged their selections and Seth stashed them in the rear seat of the pickup.

"How about lunch before we head back?" he said, indicating a tiny sandwich shop across the street. "The food's good."

They found an empty booth and ordered. Seth rested his bad leg across the seat and threw an arm along the back, watching Claire quietly.

"Why are you staring at me?" she asked.

"You've got such a nice face."

Claire was surprised at his candor. She met his gaze for a few seconds, glanced away, then looked back, clearing her throat. "You seem to be quite well-known around here. Ben yesterday, and now Raz. I didn't realize I'd hired a celebrity."

Seth's lips stretched into that crooked smile that deepened the scar in his cheek. "Would you have hired me if you had?"

Again that straightforwardness. No mock modesty or attempt at denial.

She tilted her head in thought. "I don't follow the rodeo, so I didn't recognize your name. But there's no reason I wouldn't have hired you, anyway. I was pretty hard up for help."

He looked offended. "Guess you have to settle for what you can get."

"I didn't really mean it that way."

Seth made a sucking sound between his teeth. "I suppose it's the truth, though. I wouldn't have been your first choice."

"Well, I think you'll be fine. I'm a good judge of people. And I can't thank you enough for agreeing to help me on such short notice."

Seth gave a slight nod. "We'll see how it works out. Now tell me why you don't like rodeo."

"How do you know I don't?"

"You just said you don't follow it, but it's more the way you brushed aside my suggestion we take the campers to one. Why don't we take a vote when the kids get there and see what they want to do?" When Claire didn't respond, he pressed, "Any particular reason you're vetoing this outright?"

"It's a camp, not a democracy."

Their sandwiches arrived and she hoped the food would distract him and he would forget the question. Instead, he waited patiently, his sandwich untouched.

"Delicious," she said, after taking a bite and swallowing. She dabbed her mouth with her napkin. "Really delicious."

Seth crossed his arms and raised an eyebrow. "Claire? What's your hang-up with rodeo?"

She laid her napkin beside her plate. She didn't want to discuss this, but he was obviously going to let a good sandwich go to waste if she didn't. She leaned back and crossed her arms, too. "For one thing, I don't care for the animal cruelty."

"'For one thing'? You've got a list of reasons?"

"No, not a list. And the animal thing is enough. I just don't see the need for a brutal sport that really has no value anymore."

"Pro football? Extreme fighting?"

"No animals," Claire replied. "Only stupid humans who can make their own decisions."

Seth frowned. "Didn't you grow up on a ranch? Those things go on every day. Calves being thrown and branded—and worse. Broncs being broken. Rodeo's just an extension of that. A way to hone skills, compete."

"I wasn't comfortable with ranch life, even when I was young. Maybe because my mother didn't like it at all. She divorced Dad when I was ten and took me to California. She's a horse gentler."

"Ah, that explains your rules and regulations."

Claire frowned, wondering if she'd been insulted. She placed her palms on the table and leaned toward him. "My rules and regulations are for the safety of my students and the well-being of the horses."

Seth held up a hand as if to ward off her ire. "Hey, I didn't mean anything bad by that. I understand why. And now I know where you learned it. I can't imagine your father training horses that way."

"No," Claire admitted, easing off. "He's very old school. We don't see eye to eye on horse training or much else. And for the record, I don't like the cruelty on a ranch, either, but there's not much I can do about it. My dad's sure not going to spend a lot of money on lidocaine or take the extra time to ease a calf's discomfort during cutting, even if Jon would agree."

Seth shrugged. "It's been done on ranches for years. Part of the business."

Claire leaned over the table to get even closer. "Part of the business, huh? Wonder how the calves feel about that. For that matter, how would you like to be castrated without anesthetic?"

Seth's face went a little pale. He shifted, lowering his leg from the bench seat to the floor, then leaned forward in turn, his eyes narrowing. "That's not a very nice question, but for the record, I've never given it any thought, nor do I intend to."

"I'll bet," she said.

Her lips twitched and she fought back a smile. After a long moment, she broke eye contact and gave an almost imperceptible shake of her head.

"I'm afraid you're going to be more of a handful than Micah," she said as she drew back.

Seth grunted. "Think you're up to it?"

Claire ignored that. "Eat your sandwich so we can go."

• • • •

" SO WHY DID you come back to live with your dad?" Seth asked, picking up his sandwich.

"I needed a place to stay during college. Dad wanted me back in his life, and frankly, I wanted to know him better. After school, Kaycee donated her stables for my riding school, so I stayed."

"Life's always a compromise, isn't it?"

"Seems that way."

They finished lunch, climbed into the truck and headed for Little Lobo. All the while, Seth found himself in a quandary over Claire. For the most part, he'd enjoyed being with her today. But her rejection of his rodeo idea bothered him far more than seemed warranted. Was it because it suggested she might have no interest in him, personally? He pondered that for most of the drive back.

He was accustomed to women who followed rodeo riders like remora fish. Some of them he'd kissed even before their names had penetrated his brain. Those women couldn't have cared less what happened to the animals in the arena. Mainly they were interested in the action afterward.

But Claire was no buckle bunny. From the corner of his eye he caught a glimpse of her face. Deep in thought. He saw her frown slightly and nip her lower lip. That very kissable lower lip.

He'd been so long without a woman, he was sorely tempted to stop the truck, lean over and kiss her. *Whoa, not a good idea!* Still, he wondered what she would do if he tried. Slap him? Fire him, even desperate as she was? Or would she respond, giving as good as she got? His breathing almost stopped as he weighed the danger. Might be worth the attempt.

Claire shifted to face him and caught him in the middle of that thought.

"What's on your mind now?" she asked.

Seth tumbled back to earth. Not for a million bucks would he tell her. Maybe he needed to unearth his little black book and phone one of those women he'd promised to call and never had. Might release some of the tension that had been building in him for months now. And possibly get his mind off the one woman he found interesting.

"Trying to figure out how to get you to a rodeo," he lied with a wink. "You might like it."

"Don't count on it. Besides, we've got too much work to do at camp to fit in a day trip."

What did he expect? That she would give in easily?

Wrong. Not this woman.

But then, he loved nothing better than a good challenge.

CHAPTER EIGHT

CLAIRE EXHALED HARD as she sat down at her desk. Seth was unloading the donated goods from his truck into hers so she could take everything to the ranch that night and store it in the newly refurbished dorm.

What had happened this morning? A couple of times, she'd thought Seth might try to kiss her. Maybe she had let those rugged good looks and that crooked smile trigger her imagination. Still, she didn't think it was all a fantasy....

She sat back in her chair, reflecting. What would she have done had he tried? She felt a shiver, recalling his arm around her the other day and the way he'd clasped her hand in the store today. Why was she even considering the possibility of acting on her attraction to him? He was the opposite of everything she wanted in a man. No rodeo cowboys for her! And certainly not Seth—cocky to the nth degree and possessed of a reputation she was sure she didn't want to explore.

Having him around made her think about her brother Cody more than she had in years. Her mind flashed with memories of his bright smile and laughter, along with the hurt that showed in his eyes when their father came down so hard on him for his shortcomings. The last year of his life had been truly miserable as he struggled to grow into manhood but realized he would never be the type of man their dad expected.

Because of Cody and the way his life ended, Claire wanted to help Micah Abbott more than ever. She saw his life going in the same downward spiral that Cody had suffered. She'd do her darnedest to make a difference, get him back in school, give him a reason to stay there and graduate.

But if she allowed herself to turn to mush every time Seth Morgan looked at her, she might as well fire him now and cut Micah loose.

She'd just have to steel herself and not let him get to her. Decisively, she rose to her feet. At least right now she had riding lessons that would divert her attention.

Hours later, the last lesson over and the horses tended, Claire went looking for Seth, to send him home for the day. She found him in the tack room, checking and repairing equipment they would haul to the ranch, along with Claire's lesson horses.

He looked up when he heard her come in. "Still mad at me?" he asked, rising to hang the bridle back on its hook by the door.

She shook her head. "No, and you don't have to stay past five, you know."

He glanced at his watch. "Didn't realize it was that late. How long before I earn another therapy ride?"

"Anytime. I thought you might be a little sore from yesterday."

Seth chuckled softly. "This ain't sore. I could tell you about sore."

"I'll bet you could," Claire said. "If you're ready, we can do it now."

Seth fell into step beside her as she headed for the stalls. She was careful not to be obvious as she slowed her pace to compensate for his limp.

When they reached Belle's stall, he took the lead strap and halter from the outer wall, stepped inside the enclosure and haltered the mare. Following Claire's rules, he led her out and clipped on the cross ties in the aisle. Claire brought the saddle over as he groomed the horse.

No protests from him today as he slid the pad into place and lifted the saddle onto the mare's broad back. He bent to grab the girth underneath Belle's belly.

"Ow!" He jerked upright, his hand going automatically to his thigh.

"I'll finish," Claire said.

Seth turned away, taking a halting step and muttering a few colorful words under his breath. She finished saddling in silence and after a few moments he came back.

"Sorry," he murmured, his eyes still dark with pain and embarrassment. "Stepped wrong."

"No problem. Do you still want to ride?"

"Yeah, sure. Why don't you saddle up and ride with me, instead of walking?"

"That's not exactly protocol. If something happened..."

To her surprise, instead of taking umbrage, Seth shot her a persuasive grin. "I promise not to fall off, if that helps your protocol."

Claire conceded. "Okay, we'll see how it works out." Within minutes, she had saddled Captain Jack, and led both horses to the mounting area, bringing along helmets for both of them. Seth clipped on the helmet without protest. She positioned Belle and held the bridle while he hoisted himself into the saddle and gathered the reins. Claire mounted then and nudged Jack alongside the mare. They rode in silence for a few minutes. Claire wanted to give Seth time to loosen up. He needed to, judging from the grimace of pain she could see cross his face with Belle's every stride.

When he seemed more relaxed, she said, "You're very good with children, I noticed. The little boys were showing everybody their hats after you signed them."

"Lots of those Rider kids, aren't there? And little Wyatt—you said he belongs to the couple who own the café, right?"

"Yes. Actually, he's Cimarron's nephew. He and Sarah adopted Wyatt after they got married. As for the Riders, there are seven in all. Jon's from a previous marriage."

Seth whistled softly. *Busy man.* "Divorce?"

"Widowed."

"Cute kids. And I was really impressed with Natalie and Ben. Looks like they enjoy riding, especially Natalie."

"She does, and she's stronger than she was when she started. Better balance. Her mother says she's happier, too, because she loves the horses so much."

"I can understand that," he said, giving Claire a mischievous side-long glance. "I'm happier when I'm riding something."

The glint in his eye sent a rush of heat up Claire's neck in spite of the innocent way he spoke the words. That silly song lyric "Save a horse, ride a cowboy" came to mind, and she turned her head away, afraid her face was crimson with the very thought. She fought to compose herself enough to carry on the conversation. What in the world was the matter with her?

"I'm glad to accommodate you," she said. *Shut up!* That came out wrong. Claire squirmed in the saddle and hoped he didn't catch the un-intended innuendo.

He glanced over at her and grinned broadly. "Same here."

She ignored his response, afraid she'd invite another suggestive re-mark if she spoke.

"How often do Natalie and Ben have lessons?"

"Once a week. More than that can be too stressful for these kids."

Seth rode with a natural grace, tall and straight in the saddle. Claire guided him through several stretches on horseback to help further loosen his muscles. One move that involved leaning over his injured leg elicited a soft moan, really no more than a sigh, but Claire noticed the beads of sweat on his forehead. He was hiding a good deal of pain.

"Don't overdo. Those muscles will take a while to limber up."

He exhaled hard. "It's so frustrating."

"I know. Try to let the horse do most of the work now. Maybe in a couple of days, you should get on bareback."

"Sounds like fun."

Sometimes just the way he turned a phrase made her think wanton thoughts. Warming, tingling thoughts. She snapped her wandering mind back in place. "Might be too soon at this point. You'll have to make that decision depending on how your leg feels."

He began to play around with Belle, reining her gently one way, then the other, smiling when she responded in her slow, methodical manner. He had excellent hands, easy on the bit, sensitive to the horse's reaction. Belle's ears flicked back and forth as she listened to his clucks and low-spoken commands.

"You really like horses, don't you," Claire said.

"I always have. My dad gave me my first colt, Rube, when I was only four. We grew up together, that little fellow and me. He follows me around like a puppy when...whenever I'm home."

Claire caught the hesitation in his voice but didn't want to pry. Instead she smiled and said, "Have you had enough for today? We've been riding for an hour and it's almost dark."

They circled the paddock once more and rode to the mounting block for Seth to dismount.

• • • •

He hesitated at the bottom of the long ramp, letting his pain subside as Claire led the horses to the stable, her hips swaying subtly, her long ponytail swinging with each step. All of a sudden, he didn't want to go home. While Claire hadn't exactly avoided him, she had been much more reserved since this morning, and he wanted to change that. He had this hang-up—he didn't like women not liking him!

He followed her into the stable, where she had both horses in cross ties. She was working on Jack, so Seth began to groom Belle.

"You don't have to stay," Claire said. "It won't take long to take care of them."

"Only half as long if I do my part," Seth replied. He'd come to appreciate Belle and didn't mind making her comfortable after the ride. Neither horse had worked up a lather, so it was only a matter of brushing the dust off and checking their feet.

Claire lapsed into silence as she brushed and massaged Jack's back.

"Show me what you're doing," Seth said.

"I'm relaxing his muscles." She moved to Seth's side and showed him where to press and gently knead with his fingertips.

"Like this?" He pretended he didn't catch on.

"No, use all your fingers together and move in a circle."

She grasped his hand and worked it along Belle's back. Seth went along with her, enjoying the contact fully as much as the horse did. Only, he wanted more.

"If she moves away or her skin quivers, let up and go to another spot. Try to end on a positive experience."

"I always try to," Seth said, envisioning an entirely different experience.

Claire jerked her hand off his. He continued to work on Belle, moving down her spine on one side, then the other, as Claire put Jack away. "You're going to put her into a trance," she said when she came back.

"She seems to be enjoying it."

"I need to get on the road and I have to lock up the barn. Put her away now."

"Aw, and we were having such a good time." He unsnapped Belle's halter. "Sorry, girl, blame Claire that I couldn't finish the job I started."

Claire rolled her eyes. "I'm going to lock up the office. I'll see you tomorrow."

Seth waited by his truck for her, since he'd made her late going home. They'd both parked beside the barn to free the parking lot for the two adjacent businesses.

A cool breeze drifted down from the mountains, sweet with night fragrances. Seth was tired, but it was a good tired from work and riding, nothing like the fatigue he'd dealt with for months now. Claire crossed the stable yard, her form almost lost in the deepening dusk. She jumped when she realized he was still there.

"I thought you'd gone."

"Nope. Still here."

"Why?"

He shrugged. "It's late. I didn't want you to close up all alone."

"I do it all the time."

"Doesn't mean it's right. Will you be okay getting home?" Seth stuck the tips of his fingers into his jeans pockets. "I can follow you if you want, since I'm the one who kept you late."

Claire laughed softly. "Seth, I've driven home lots later than this. I had a night class at MSU for three semesters and got in well after midnight. Next time, cut down on Belle's massage."

"I don't know how she'll take that. She looked pretty happy."

"I'm sure. Well, I need to get going."

"Claire..." Seth said, reaching toward her.

She stepped back. He let his hand drop.

"Are you afraid of me?" he asked.

"No, of course not."

"Then why do you back away every time I come near?"

"Seth, you and I have a business relationship. That's all it can be."

"That's all it is, as far as I'm concerned. But I don't understand what you've got against me. Just because I rodeo, you don't like me?"

"It's not that I don't like you, but you're always making suggestive remarks, and I don't quite know where you're coming from."

"Okay, I'll can the remarks. I'm only joking around. Libby calls me on it, too, sometimes. But then, some women like it."

"Well, I don't."

The thought of several weeks of this cool treatment made Seth wish he hadn't been so quick to commit. He'd never been one to mince words, either. "Frankly, I don't care much for being where I'm not wanted."

"You promised me the whole summer."

He couldn't read her expression, but her attitude made him angry. He hadn't let her personal views stand between them being civil, but apparently she had. "I signed on to the camp to help you out, and I'm not going to leave you hanging. But you could at least lighten up a little."

He climbed INTO the truck and drove away, leaving her standing there, realizing that he was more right than wrong.

She thought about the problem all the way home. Even tried to call her mom but got the answering machine. Claire left a message that she'd call later. There was no telling where her mom was this week. She stayed busy giving horse-training seminars and clinics all over the country.

Clint was sitting on the front steps of his house when Claire drove up. Although he'd never admit it, she knew he was watching for her, worried that something had happened. None of them would ever get over that night spent waiting for Cody.

"Hey, Dad. Sorry I'm late."

"Figured you got busy. Or maybe went out to dinner with Morgan."

She sat down beside him. Sometimes getting a word out of him was like pulling teeth. Claire was glad he was in a fatherly mood tonight.

"I don't think Seth and I will be going out to dinner."

Clint snorted. "Well, not once you get out here. Nowhere to go but Rosie's kitchen."

"That's not what I mean. I...we...he's a little miffed at me right now."

"Honey, you're not on him already about that bull riding, are you?"

"He brought it up at lunch today." Why did she feel defensive telling the truth? "He wanted to take the campers to the Livingston Roundup and I nixed the idea. He asked me what I had against rodeo."

Clint looked at her askance. "You told him?"

"I told him I didn't like the mistreatment of the animals."

Her dad didn't comment.

"The rest is none of his business," Claire said. "But I'll admit I was not in a good mood this afternoon, and he took it a little personally."

"He'll get over it. Men don't dwell on that kind of thing long."

"I hope not. I don't want us to be on bad terms all summer. It won't be good for the campers."

"Or you. Or Seth." Clint stood, stretched his arms over his head and yawned. "You might as well come inside and warm up the plate Rosie left."

"Oh, Rosie was here again?"

"Yep, she stayed to eat this time."

Claire followed him into the house. "Are you and Rosie up to something?"

"Would you mind if we were?" Clint asked hesitantly. "I mean...your mother and all."

"Mom's gone on with her life. She wouldn't care. I'd like for you to have someone, and Rosie's wonderful. If it makes you happy, I'm all for it."

Clint gave her a peck on the cheek. "We'll see what happens." He chuckled. "I'm curious how you manage with Seth. Better watch your step and remember he's going to be gone again at the end of the summer."

Claire turned from the microwave, where she'd put the plate to heat. "What are you talking about?"

"He's been a big deal in bull riding for the last few years. I remember him from some high school rodeos I worked back when Jon raised bucking bulls. He's a damn good rider. I always..." Clint's voice drifted off. He cleared his throat. "Anyway, he's been at the top for a long time and I imagine he's used to women falling all over him."

"Well, he can forget about that with me."

"I imagine that's what has him stumped, wondering why you're different from the rest," Clint said with a wink. "And I bet he don't give up easy, either."

CHAPTER NINE

CLAIRE AND SETH WERE BUSY the rest of the week. Each morning began with his therapy ride, which he seemed to enjoy more as his discomfort eased. Claire was impressed by the effort he put into improvement. He was fearless on horseback, even with his injury, and never hesitated to attempt her challenging exercises. On Friday he rode bareback for the first time, and Claire was pleased with the progress he'd made in only a few sessions.

He asked again about bringing Rube to the ranch, and this time Claire agreed wholeheartedly. As her camp assistant, Seth proved a willing worker and could fix anything, including the faulty safety lights on the back of her old horse trailer. He was a horseman at heart and Claire appreciated his caring attention to Belle and the other animals. Within a few days' time, he couldn't walk down the row of stalls without a chorus of welcoming nickers.

Most surprising to Claire, considering the attitude he copped with her at first, was his rapport with the youngsters. The Rider boys and Wyatt came by the stable every afternoon that week, and Seth always made time for them, assigning them easy chores or telling them anecdotes about bull riding. He also made a point of observing Ben and Natalie's lessons.

Claire watched with interest and a bit of trepidation as Ben's hero worship increased. She didn't like Seth filling his head with impossible dreams, but Ben's mother was thrilled with her son's newfound enthusiasm. While several of her therapeutic riders were taking the summer off due to vacations and other commitments, Natalie and Ben wanted to continue, so Claire agreed to teach them at the ranch, between sessions with the campers.

On Saturday Seth came to work with the backseat of his truck packed with most of his belongings from Libby's house. Using her two-horse trailer and a livestock rig, Claire and Seth moved the horses to their summer home. Claire had worked with Jon and Cimarron to gut one of the old broodmare barns and redesign it according to her specifications. There was a large open area at one end and a cluster of stalls at the other. A roomy opening led to a large pasture where the horses could roam and graze yet have access at will to the barn.

"I'll keep them confined a few days," Claire explained as she and Seth worked to settle the animals into their stalls, "then give them the freedom to explore the pasture and common area. I love being able to allow them to herd naturally. The horses are more relaxed and that helps my challenged riders."

"That's me," Seth said, faking a pitiful voice. "One of your challenged riders."

"Oh, get a life and stop whining," she retorted. "Your leg is getting better every day."

"Yep, this therapeutic riding might get me back on a bull in record time."

Claire didn't respond.

"Or maybe not, is that what you're thinking?" Seth said, resetting his hat on his head.

"No, I was wondering why you'd be crazy enough to *want* to get on another bull. It's one of those self-destructive guy things I don't understand."

Seth pulled a face. "Well, I am a guy, in case you haven't noticed. But it's deeper than that. It's what I do well. Bull riding is a part of me. I can't imagine myself without it." He leaned on the top rail of one of the stalls and looked around at Claire. "What if tomorrow something happened and you couldn't work with horses anymore, at all?"

That possibility had never crossed her mind. Sheer panic welled up in her at the thought. But what she did was different from bull riding. It was positive, healing, not life-threatening.

"Look at Natalie and Ben," she said. "They struggle every day with their physical challenges. Why would you even chance deliberately putting yourself in that position?"

"I don't really see the correlation. They can't help the afflictions they were born with, but they're doing the best they can. If I was crippled, I'd have to do the same thing. And I guess I will, if I can't ride again after this leg heals."

"Will that be so bad? I mean, you'll have to go on to something else eventually. I can't believe there are any really old bull riders. Could be a reason. And maybe this is a blessing in disguise."

Seth blew out a long, soft breath. "Blessing? If I can't ride again..." He shook his head and looked away. "I don't want to think about it. It would be like cutting out my heart. The worst thing that could happen to me."

"No." Claire stared at him, unable to believe what she was hearing. "You could be killed or maimed for life."

"I know what I face every time I get on a bull, Claire. It's what I'll face if I *can't* get on one that scares me half to death."

Claire couldn't offer him the solace he sought, and the silence between them grew heavy. Finally she said, "Why don't I show you the bunkhouse we're going to use, and you can move your things in?"

"Good idea." He seemed happy to change the subject.

"Is Libby okay with you moving out?"

"She'd never admit it, but I'll bet she's glad to be rid of me. I've been a lot of work for her."

"I never heard her complain about you."

"Libby doesn't complain, but she sure threatened me this time."

"Threatened you how?"

"Said she was going to sic our dad on me if I didn't get my *butt* busy this summer." Seth chuckled. "And my sister *never* says 'butt.'"

Claire laughed at that. "I agree. Libby's got the cleanest mouth I know."

They approached a large building at a distance from the barn. A broad covered porch ran the length of the front, with five doors opening onto it.

She opened the far left door. The clean scents of fresh wood and new paint enveloped them as they entered. "This will be the activities room and the dining hall. Sarah donated all the food for the summer, and Rosie's going to cook for us."

A bank of cabinets and bookshelves flanked one wall of the large room. Several dozen books and stacks of games in boxes were already in place. Uncovered windows on the other three walls let in ample light. A wide, long table in the center would seat up to twelve people.

Seth followed Claire back out and to the next door. "This is the boys' room," she told him. "Table and chairs for activities." She flipped the light switch. "Plenty of light for reading. The bathroom is over here."

She turned on the lights there and showed Seth the multiple showers, toilet stalls and lavatories. Slatted benches like those in a health club lined the short wall. She tapped the wood paneling.

"Nice strong wall between the boys' and girls' quarters. This used to be one big bunkhouse, but Jon let Cimarron remodel it completely. I'll be able to use it every year for camp. I'm hoping to be able to expand each summer, to maybe a maximum of twelve teenagers. The girls' area is a mirror image of this side. You and I each have a separate bedroom, with an office area, bathroom, and an entrance from our rooms to the front porch."

"Darn," Seth said, making a disappointed face. "We could save space and water by sharing one."

"Too late. I moved my things in last night. There's also a door opening from our apartments into the dorm rooms, which I expect to be unlocked at all times and open at night. I don't want any opportunity for bullying—or escape."

She led Seth into his room through that door. His space had a desk, computer table, bookcase and small filing cabinet, in addition to a bed, bureau and nightstand. The bathroom was compact but had all the necessities.

"Will this do?" she asked when they were on the porch again.

"Sure. It's luxurious compared to some places I've stayed. And I guess it's roomier if we don't share."

Claire rolled her eyes. "Seth, stop with the wisecracks. Why don't you get unpacked and come to my dad's house for dinner around seven? I'll have him grill steaks."

"Sounds like a plan."

• • • •

SETH SOON HAD HIS new lodgings in order. The walls were of unfinished wood, like the rest of the bunkhouse, with the sweet smell of fir still hanging in the air. The scent and warmth of the wood took him back to his childhood, when his father had built the new ranch house to accommodate his growing family.

Seth's room had looked a lot like this one, with a window that overlooked a lush mountain vista, and a bunk bed for him and his ten-year-old brother. Lane had protested vehemently about being stuck with the "baby" just because he was the next-youngest boy. In the end, Seth and he had bonded more closely than any of their brothers.

After showering, shaving and changing clothes, Seth still had a few minutes to kill, so he headed outside to explore. The large ranch was well equipped and well organized. Breeding and calving barns were sterile with the most up-to-date equipment. He'd love to have an operation like this one day, focused more on breeding than the general ranching his father had done.

He approached a corral where several horses were milling. The animals stopped and pricked their ears toward him when he approached. A few months ago, any of these would have made a good mount, but now...well, he could barely keep his seat on Belle. These youngsters would have him on the ground in a heartbeat.

Seth dialed his cell phone and waited for his brother to answer.

"Lane, how's it going?" he said, talking as he walked slowly toward Claire's father's house.

"Fine. You?"

"Doing better. Are you still bringing Rube up for me tomorrow?"

"Planned on it. Dad wants to ride along."

"No way. I'm not in the mood to have it out with him."

"Sooner or later, you're going to have to."

"Maybe. But not now."

"His feelings are going to be hurt if I say no."

"I doubt that, but I do need Rube, so make some excuse. I swear I'll come home soon and try to patch things up."

"I'm going to hold you to that."

"Whatever. So I'm at the Rider ranch...." Seth gave his brother directions.

"Okay. I should be there late afternoon, barring problems."

"Don't bring Dad," Seth insisted again.

"I'll do my best."

Seth crossed the expansive open area separating the barns and outbuildings from the ranch house, bunkhouse and other residential structures. Clint's place lay beyond the grassy bounds of a narrow valley, all but hidden from view by a grove of larch and spruce.

Claire waved from a wide back deck where she was setting a picnic table with plates and utensils. Smoke wafted from a grill, bringing with it the mouthwatering aroma of grilling meat.

"Steaks will be ready in a few minutes," Claire said. "Did you get settled?"

"I did. Then I took a walk around the barns."

"Nice place, isn't it?"

"Very. How long has your father managed it?"

"All his life, basically. And his father before him. Family tradition, you might say."

"So you're going to take over next?" Seth asked lightly.

To his surprise, Claire grew solemn. She shook her head. "No. I'm afraid the tradition ended with..." Her voice trailed off.

"With what?"

Before she could answer, a tall, lanky man stepped through the back door with a couple of bottles of beer in one hand and a glass of wine in the other. He set them down on the table.

Quickly, Claire made the introductions, and the two men shook hands cordially.

"I'm glad to finally meet you, Seth," Clint said. "I've heard a lot about you over the years."

"Hmm, that could be bad, depending on who's doing the telling."

Clint laughed. "No need to worry. My memory gets shorter as the years go by." He handed the wine to Claire, then a beer to Seth, grabbing the other for himself. "That was a pretty bad wreck you had earlier this year. One of my hands was there that night and said he thought you might be dead when they carted you off."

"I thought I was, too," Seth admitted, taking a pull on the beer. "What's the name of the hand?"

"Chance Shelton."

"Chance was riding that night. He works here now?"

"Yep. You two friends?"

"Not really. Different personalities."

Clint nodded. "I can see that."

Seth didn't remember much about the ride anymore, except what came back in nightmares, but he'd never forgotten the evil glint in Rotten's eye. "That bull's hurt another couple of riders since then," he stated.

The deep crow's-feet around the weathered cowhand's eyes gave him a permanent squint. "They ought to retire him before he kills somebody. Money, that's about all that matters anymore, I guess. When are you getting back on?"

A cold tremor ran through Seth like an ill omen. The ache in his leg was getting worse the longer he stood on it, a nagging reminder that nobody could predict the future. "As soon as the doc releases me. Hopefully in time to make finals."

Clint grunted. "Don't go back too soon. There's always next year. Mess that leg up again and you might be out for good."

"I know. I'm waiting."

Barely. Every day the urge grew stronger to challenge himself, to prove that he could still compete. He felt like a bull caught in the chute, dying to get free, ready to explode, to buck that monkey-man off his back, but nobody would open the gate. Seth's gate wouldn't open until the doctor said so, and right now he said no way. In fact, Doc had said *never*.

Never just wasn't an option.

"Claire's riding lessons are helping," Seth admitted.

Clint looked at his daughter with pride. "She's a wonder at healing. You couldn't be in better hands."

"I've been thinking the same thing," Seth said.

· · · ·

WHY WAS IT, Claire wondered as she listened to the two men talk, that the most innocuous words from this man's mouth could give her butterflies? More the way he said them than the words themselves. With that subtle, smoldering undertone that made her wonder what he actually *meant*.

Following Clint to the barbecue while he turned the steaks, Seth stood to one side with his feet slightly apart, hands resting lightly on his hips. It was the exact pose of the sexy, full-length photo of him dressed in his full regalia, posted on his Web site. Claire had done quite a bit of research on him, finding mostly statistics and career highlights, but she understood now why so many people in the area knew him. He'd won several major bull riding events over the past few years and was a much bigger name in the sport than she'd imagined.

Maybe *that* explained the attitude. Not that she was cutting him any slack because of his fame.

She'd also read the reports of his horrific accident and agreed with her father that Seth was lucky to be alive. So many people would love to have his sound body and mind, yet he seemed heedless of the precious gift he'd been given. She was more than amazed that he fully intended to risk an eight-second thrill ride on a bull again despite the doctor's warning.

Claire went inside to make the salad. When she returned with salad bowl and condiments, she was stopped in the doorway by an unusual sound: her father laughing. A big, full-bellied laugh. He was listening to Seth tell some bull riding tale.

"...so they couldn't corral the bulls inside the coliseum, and they were running them in from outside, into the chutes."

The fire burned bright in Seth's eyes as he talked, she noticed, and his broad grin cut the dimple-scar deep in his cheek. "It was cold as hell and snowing, and the bulls still had an inch of snow on their backs when we had to get on. Frozen fingers, slippery ropes and wet butts—not a good combination for staying in the middle."

Her father shook his head. "Never would've thought about having to worry about snow inside like that. I did a little saddle bronc riding, but that's about all. Gotta say I'll leave that to you young bucks."

"I did a lot of bronc busting for my father when I was at home," Seth said. "But I always like riding the bulls better."

"Your dad a rider?"

Seth shook his head. "No. None of my four brothers, either. The rest went to college like they were supposed to. Two brothers moved away and two went back to the ranch to help Dad. My sister teaches school. You might say I turned out to be the black sheep in the family."

"Hand me that platter there, would you? What got you started on bulls?"

Seth held out the big plate so Clint could deposit the steaks. "My brothers thought it would make a good joke to put me on a young bull they'd raised for 4-H. I was about six or seven. They tied a rope around the girth and told me to hold on. That bull went berserk, with me hanging on for dear life. The boys couldn't catch him and we went halfway across the pasture before I fell off. They got a thrashing, but that's all I ever wanted to do afterward." He paused. "Still all I ever want to do."

"I reckon you'll be back at it then, no matter what."

"I sure plan on it."

When Seth caught Claire watching from the doorway, the light in his eyes dimmed and the enthusiasm left his voice. She headed for the picnic table.

"Are we ready to eat, Claire?" Clint said, glancing from her to Seth. "Salad and bread done?"

"Yep. On the table," she answered.

They sat down, Clint on one side and Claire and Seth across from him.

"So camp starts tomorrow?" Clint asked. She knew he wouldn't continue the rodeo talk with her there.

"Yes, the campers come tomorrow afternoon." She turned to Seth. "I'm going to need you to pick up Micah, if you don't mind. He doesn't have a ride out here and doesn't want to come, anyway—" she smiled grimly "—so I don't want to give him any excuse to back out."

"Sure, that's not a problem. My brother's bringing my horse tomorrow, but he won't get here until later in the afternoon."

As they ate, the conversation turned to other subjects. Seth and Clint compared notes on ranching, and Claire was content to listen, glad that the two got along. After helping her dad clean up, she and Seth walked back to the bunkhouse together.

A cool breeze drifted down the valley lit by a three-quarter moon, sweet with night fragrances. She stared at the large bunkhouse and tried to picture the kids who would soon be living there, including the troubled boy at a crossroads in his young life.

"Claire, you look a world away."

"I guess I'm a little nervous about camp. I want to help these kids, not set them back."

"No way you're going to set them back. I've seen how you interact with your riders. You'll be just as good with the campers."

"I've dealt with mentally and physically challenged children for a long time, but I've never done anything like this."

"That makes two of us. I guess we'll just have to feel our way along."

Claire tried to convince herself that the statement was another of the sort of remarks Seth made, not deliberately suggestive. She stopped outside her door when they reached the bunkhouse porch, and turned to him, seeking his face in the dim light of a rising moon. "I guess so."

"Everything's going to work out okay," he said, pushing a strand of hair off her face. She pulled back as his fingers brushed her cheek.

"Such optimism," she said, her better judgment screaming for her to say good-night, open her door and disappear inside. She didn't want to hurt his feelings, but she didn't intend to start anything they couldn't finish. There would never be anything between them if he intended to return to bull riding.

"That's me, ever the optimist. Besides, I've seen your determination," he said, lowering his head toward her, as if he might kiss her. "If you can get a helmet on me, you can do anything."

"I think we need to say good-night." Claire reached behind her for the doorknob.

Seth was near enough that she caught the scent of him, an intoxicating mix of aftershave, clean cotton and male pheromones that made her want to stay when she knew better.

He shifted even nearer. She found the doorknob.

• • • •

Seth sensed her uncertainty and saw her hand groping for the door. The more time he spent around Claire, the more he was attracted to her—and the less he was willing to accept the idea that she might not like him at all simply because of what he did for a living.

He reached around her and caught her hand before she could slip into her room. She tried to pull away, but he held fast.

"Let go, Seth," she ordered.

He never had been much for taking orders. He did, however, loosen his grip enough that she could pull free if she really wanted to. To his surprise, she didn't. He liked the feel of her hand in his, small, strong, her palm callused from hard work with her horses. He wasn't sure what he wanted from Claire. He wasn't particularly looking for a long-term relationship, and he certainly didn't expect a one-night stand from a woman like her. But he really wanted to kiss her in the here and now.

He moved closer.

She edged back until she was pressed against the door.

He drew up short, frustrated. "What's wrong with a good-night kiss? Is it just the bull riding you hold against me, or something else?"

"I don't hold anything against you," she said. "Why would I?"

"You act like I've got two heads or something."

"Because I didn't fall at your feet like a groupie?"

Seth gave her a wry look. "Well, yeah, that's one thing."

"Come on, you've got to be kidding." She slid her hand out of his grasp. Did he only imagine she let her fingertips linger in his?

Seth braced a hand on either side of the door behind her and said softly, "A guy can get used to that sort of adoration."

Claire laughed. "You don't say? Sorry, I'm not that type."

"What type are you, Claire?" he asked, leaning toward her.

"Probably not one you'd want," she said.

"You might be surprised, darlin'. If you'd give me a chance, I might prove to be *your* type."

"I doubt that. Like I told you before, I'm a pretty good judge of people and I know a cowboy when I see one."

"And that's all bad?"

"I can't handle that sort of mentality. Everything's black-and-white, no middle ground."

She made no effort to move away from him, and his heartbeat quickened with the powerful urge to kiss her, to pull her close and know what her body felt like against his.

"Maybe I'm different." He brushed her lips lightly with his.

She gasped and put a hand on his chest. "Seth!"

"I love the way you say my name."

"Seth...We shouldn't do this."

"Why? We're adults. There's nothing wrong—"

"Everything's wrong!"

"Claire..." He tried to draw her back into his arms.

She pushed him away. "No. We cannot become involved this way."

His voice hardened. "Give me a good reason."

"We have to carry on a professional relationship. I'm your employer."

"That's temporary." Again he reached for her.

"No. You don't understand. Even after camp ends, we have nothing. Nothing, Seth."

"We might, if you give us a chance. Unless you try you'll never know. You might find out a bull rider's not all that bad."

Tears filled Claire's eyes, but she blinked them away and shook her head.

"Claire..."

"Please go. I can't do this. I—I can't let myself...."

"Tell me why. I'm a good guy, you know," he said, then smiled. "In spite of what you might have heard."

"It's not *who* you are, Seth. It's *what* you are."

"That's not fair. I can't change the past."

"No, but I heard you tell my dad you were going back to bull riding, and I can't take that chance."

"What chance?" Seth said his voice a pitch higher with exasperation. "I'll be the one taking the chances, riding the bulls. I don't understand what you mean."

"The chance I'll be taking is waiting every weekend for you to come home—and hoping you'll be in one piece. And what if you don't come home one—" Claire broke off her sentence. She couldn't go there right now.

She steeled herself and opened the door. "It will never work, Seth."

Seth leaned close and gave her that crooked grin. She felt his breath on her face when he whispered, "Wait and see. Chances are it will."

He tipped his hat to her, turned on his heel and strode off.

CHAPTER TEN

SETH TOOK A COLD SHOWER in the tiny bathroom and went to bed.

He could hear her moving about on the other side of the wall, which only made him ache to hold her. After a few hours of tossing and turning, he fell into a restless sleep, waking again when he heard a rooster crow in the distance. Pale light filtered in around the window shade.

Claire hadn't set any specific time to get started today, but Seth knew he wouldn't fall asleep again. He dressed and went outside into the nippy morning air. The shadows were receding quickly as the sun's rays topped the mountains.

He wasn't sure what to do about breakfast but figured as a last resort he could find fast food on the way to pick up Micah later in the morning. The horses needed to be fed, so he got busy in the barn. Halfway through the process, Claire came in. Seth held his breath, waiting for her to break the silence.

"Good morning," she said, her voice pleasant but remote.

"Morning," Seth answered, taking her cue. "Thought I'd get this chore out of the way."

"Thanks, I'll help you finish. Breakfast in an hour in the bunkhouse dining room. Rosie starts cooking for us today."

"Good. I was wondering about that."

Seth didn't like the distance between them as they worked their way down the row of stalls. He wanted to know the real reason she didn't want anything to do with him. It couldn't be just that he was cowboy.

"Claire, about last night..."

She turned to him, her face ashen, her hazel eyes flashing. "Don't," she said harshly. "I told you to forget it."

Seth glared at her. "No problem. What else do you need done before I go for Micah?"

"I'm not sure you should pick him up with that attitude. I'll send one of the hands for him."

Seth caught her by the arm as she stalked past him. He pulled her around to face him. "No you won't, unless you fire me on the spot. I'm going to do my job right, whether you like me or not."

Claire narrowed her eyes at him. "You'd better." She jerked away and walked toward the door. "Breakfast should be ready soon."

"I'm not hungry," Seth muttered.

If she heard him, she didn't give any indication. Seth cursed under his breath and wanted to kick something, but he'd long ago learned to control those urges. The cameras were always rolling behind the chutes, as well as in the arena. Any outward show of temper or disappointment would be replayed and dissected for weeks by commentators and on the Internet.

So he went to his room, found a map to Micah's house in the manual Claire had given him and headed into town.

• • • •

AFTER SETH DROVE OFF, Claire fought to get her emotions under control. She could not fly off the handle at him in front of the kids. And she didn't want to fire him, because that would mean losing Micah, and Jason, too. She had to keep her cool, make Seth keep his. Just for a few weeks, she told herself. Just a few weeks.

Seth had the power to drive her out of her mind and tear down her defenses, to the point she didn't care what happened next. But she had to protect her heart. If Seth decided to go back to bull riding, Claire feared she would spend a lifetime terrified that he'd never come home again. Just like Cody. She wasn't sure all the love in the world could diminish that worry, and the best way to avoid it was not to fall in love with Seth in the first place.

Thank goodness she didn't have time to dwell on the problem. She had plenty to do before her campers arrived early afternoon. She spent the rest of the morning doing groundwork with the horses Jon had loaned her. Each camper would be assigned a horse to use for the duration. Claire had riding activities planned that would allow the teenagers to learn to depend on their horses, as well as one another.

She was pleased with the new animals and, as usual, could feel a oneness with each of them. Once they understood what she wanted, they responded immediately to her soft commands to walk, trot, canter or stop. Her mother had an uncanny bond with horses, and Claire had inherited that connection.

When she finished, she introduced the ranch horses to her school horses, and observed their behavior for a few minutes before turning the former into an adjacent pasture.

While her camp was small this first year, and not a traditional wilderness program, she was sure the young people would benefit from their interaction with the horses, as well as the chance to make responsible decisions and experience success. Claire had high hopes for expanding her camp each year. She planned to bring in trained counselors—ones who wouldn't leave her in the lurch like Barry.

She returned to the bunkhouse, where she laid out orientation materials for each camper, including camp rules, first-aid instructions and a list of chores the participants would choose to do to earn points. She was done in plenty of time and waited impatiently for the teens to arrive. She needed them here to keep her mind off Seth.

Claire had always thought that working with horses and young people would be enough to satisfy her for life, especially after a couple of unhappy experiences with boyfriends in college. Now Seth had ignited a restlessness in her, and she didn't like it.

At last she heard a vehicle coming down the gravel road. She took a deep breath, pushed the negative thoughts aside and went out to greet her first camper.

· · · ·

SETH LOCATED the ramshackle trailer at the end of a dirt road several miles on the other side of Little Lobo. When he pulled up, a tall, well-built, dark-haired teenager rushed out the front door, letting the torn screen door flap back into place. Seth stepped down from the truck.

"I'm coming!" Micah shouted to him, then turned back toward the interior of the house. "No, Mom! You stay inside. I'm gone."

A woman's voice carried on the quiet air. "But, Micah, I want to meet—"

"No!" he roared. The teen rushed to the truck, threw his duffel bag in the back and jumped in the cab. "Let's go, okay?" he said desperately.

"I'll be happy to meet your mom," Seth said.

"No, just please drive! Let's get out of here!" Micah's dark eyes pleaded with Seth, and he looked mortified when his mother stepped onto the porch.

Seth debated the right thing to do: don't embarrass the kid any further or show respect to the mother. Seth blew out a short sigh. His own mother had ground politeness into him with the diligence of a drill sergeant.

"Sorry, kid," he said to Micah. "You wait here for a minute."

He got out of the truck and approached the porch, where a bedraggled-looking woman stood with her arms around her waist, apparently holding in place the tattered bathrobe she wore.

"Ma'am," Seth said, tipping his hat with a couple of fingers. "I'm Seth Morgan, one of the camp administrators."

"Thank you for coming for Micah," she said in a hoarse voice. "He needs to get away from here for a while."

"Yes, ma'am. We're going to see that he has a good summer."

She nodded and glanced at her son, who was slumped down in the seat of the truck. Her eyes softened, but Seth could see the unhappiness in their depths. "Guess he's ready to go. I hope he won't give you any trouble."

"Don't worry, ma'am. We'll take care of him."

She nodded and Seth returned to the truck. As he put it in reverse and turned around, he noticed she'd gone inside, but was watching through the screen door. She had her hand to her mouth, and he knew she was crying.

As he pulled off the dirt road onto the main road, Seth noted the school-bus stop.

"You have to walk all the way down here for the bus?" he asked. The dirt road was over a mile long, and he hadn't seen a vehicle at the trailer other than a weed-riddled, broken-down pickup.

"Yeah," Micah said. "The limo's at the repair shop."

Seth decided to ignore the insolence. Still, considering the kid's attitude, Seth was surprised he bothered to go to school at all.

Micah ignored Seth the rest of the way to town. Claire's only mandate was to get the boy to the camp, not to force him to talk, so he concentrated on the road and let Micah stew.

"This town's a dump," Micah grumbled as they passed through Little Lobo.

"You know some better place?" Seth said without looking at him.

"Anywhere else."

Seth pondered that awhile. "I guess I felt that way when I first came here, but just about any place is what you make of it."

"Yeah, and you saw what my family's made of it. My mother's a total loser. And my dad's worse."

"I didn't see your dad," Seth said.

"No, not likely to. He's in prison."

"That's tough."

"Yeah, well, and now Mom's taken a nosedive. It just..." Micah shook his head. "Just sucks, that's all. So what's this damn camp all about, anyway? You think you can fix me in a matter of weeks?"

"I think we can give you a break from your troubles, at least. What you take away from it is up to you."

"What's the point? I go back to the same hellhole when camp's over." Micah propped a scruffy tennis shoe on the dashboard.

"The first thing you'd better do is lose the language. And take your foot off my dashboard."

"Like hell," Micah mumbled. He frowned, staring straight ahead, and didn't move a muscle. Seth gave him another minute, then slammed on the brakes enough that Micah jerked forward against the seat belt, and his foot slipped off the dash to the floor.

"My truck doesn't get abused and I don't like bad language from kids," Seth growled. "Keep that in mind."

Micah didn't speak to him again the rest of the way to the ranch, and Seth didn't consider it a great loss. Claire would probably fire him the next day or two, anyway, so why worry about this kid?

Seth parked the truck and got out. Micah grabbed his duffel and followed him to the dining area of the bunkhouse, where Claire and the three other campers sat chatting. Seth opened the screen door and indicated to Micah to go in. He could almost smell the anxiety in the boy.

But to Seth's surprise, Micah's expression lightened and he almost smiled when he went inside. Seth followed his gaze to sixteen-year-old Annie, a pretty girl with long blond hair. Annie took one look at Micah, however, turned up her nose and looked away. Micah's face hardened again and he squared his shoulders as Claire approached.

"Welcome, Micah. We're so glad to have you here this summer."

Micah mumbled something unintelligible.

Claire ignored his ill manners and introduced Micah and Seth to the others. Micah knew Annie because she was in his classes at school, but showed little interest in the two other campers, Jason and Mary Lou.

"Okay, we know each other from school. Can I go to my room now?" Micah said.

"Not yet," Claire said with a patient smile. "We were waiting for you before we got started with the orientation and paperwork."

"Wonderful," he muttered, slinging his duffel into a corner and slumping down apart from the others.

"Move closer, please," Claire told him.

Micah stayed where he was. Seth cleared his throat and nodded toward the empty place near Jason. Micah returned a killing glare, but after a few seconds of challenge, moved to join the others.

This kid needed a strap before he'd be ready for kid gloves, Seth thought, straddling the picnic bench at the end of the table Micah had vacated. But probably his job was secure as long as Micah stayed at camp.

The campers filled out several pages of paperwork. The last segment of the personal information form was a short essay on what they wanted to achieve at camp. Seth could see Micah's paper well enough to read the large scrawled letters that spelled *NOTHING*. Claire had picked a doozy with this one.

Seth watched her collect the papers, taking Micah's last; he saw her eyes fall on the cryptic word in the bottom section. She showed no reaction. Stacking the papers neatly, she put them in her file.

"You'll find a list of rules in your packet, as well as posted on the bulletin board."

"How are you going to make us obey them?" Micah said, lounging back and eyeing Claire defiantly. "You can't hit us—it's against the law."

"Why would anyone hit you? But you will behave if you decide to stay here, Micah. We earn our rewards by good behavior and lose them by bad behavior."

"What rewards?"

The kid's cocky, belligerent attitude toward Claire infuriated Seth. But he held his tongue.

She moved to a long table at the front of the room and lifted a light-weight tarp to reveal the trove of brand-new items she and Seth had picked up in Livingston.

A collective "wow" went up from the campers. Even Micah's mouth fell slack.

"So all that's ours?" he asked. "All those boots, hats and back-packs?"

"Yep. But you have to *earn* the right to keep them by doing ranch and camp chores. The boots and hats are different. You have to earn the right to *get* them."

"What chores?" Annie said.

"There's a sign-up sheet for chores on the bulletin board."

"So we earn points and get these things, like, to take home when camp's over?" Mary Lou asked.

"Yes, as long as you obey the rules. If you break a rule, either points or a piece of your gear will be taken away and will have to be earned back through extra work."

"Figures," Micah muttered.

"It's only fair," Claire responded. "The good things in life don't come cheap or easy, Micah. You'll earn your way here or do without."

"Bitch," Micah said under his breath.

Claire either didn't hear or chose to ignore Micah. Seth, however, chose not to ignore it. He slid down the bench toward the boy.

"If I hear another word like that come out of your mouth, you won't keep *any* of those things. Do you understand?"

Micah shot him a look from narrowed eyes but didn't retaliate.

"Good," Seth said. Claire had begun to go over the rules and camp activities. Seth jerked his chin toward her. "Now pay attention."

When she finished, Micah snorted. "Can I go home now?"

"Sure, if that's what you want," Claire said without missing a beat. "There's the door. Seth can drive you." She turned to the others. "Now,

I'm going to hand out your clothes. They should fit, since I got your sizes from school. Annie..."

Claire had picked up a plastic bag from the table that had Annie's name on the label. The girl took it back to her table and opened it.

"Omigosh!" she squealed, pulling out a pink Western shirt, two T-shirts with camp logos, and two pair of jeans. In the bottom of the bag she found a belt and socks. She looked up at Claire with wide blue eyes. "This is all mine?"

"Yes, that's your incentive to stay with the program."

"Look, Mary Lou," Annie said, holding up the shirt. "My favorite color."

Mary Lou admired the garment. Seth remembered from her chart that Mary Lou had anger-management problems and was prone to outbursts, but right now she was far from angry, and turned eagerly toward Claire, who held out her packet.

Inside, Mary Lou found the same items, and an ice-blue shirt that she, too, proclaimed to be her favorite color. Seth understood now why Claire had gathered so much information on the campers. The happy excitement that resulted was worth every effort.

"Jason," Claire called, handing him his bag.

The boy returned to his seat, looked around self-consciously before he opened the bag, and didn't pull any of the stuff out to show. Only a year younger than the others, Jason looked and acted much less mature. He was at camp because of self-esteem issues. Seth had helped Claire pack the bags and knew there was a bright red plaid shirt in Jason's.

"Micah."

She held out his package. Micah didn't move, and neither did Claire. The standoff lasted a good thirty seconds.

"What if I don't want any of your sh—stuff?" Micah said, shooting a sidelong glance at Seth.

"It makes no difference to me, Micah, or any of the others," Claire replied. "I'm offering it to you early to give you a head start, but you're welcome to do things the hard way, if you want."

· · · ·

He sat, undecided, for a long minute. *Hell, no need to do things the hard way, if I'm going to be stuck here.* He shuffled to the front of the class to take the booty from Claire.

A flicker of excitement sparked through him as he opened the bag, but he refused to show it, instead pressing his lips together and trying to look indifferent. He peered in, saw a flash of bright color and almost smiled. He pulled out the royal-blue shirt just enough to rub the soft material between his fingers and see the brilliant fabric in better light.

He'd never blurt it out like the girls, but it was a good-looking shirt. He reached deep into the bag to touch the stiffness of the jeans. No thrift-store purchase like he normally had to wear. These jeans were so new he could still smell the dye. And beneath them he could feel the smooth leather of a belt. He hadn't had new clothes since his daddy was sent off.

Okay, so maybe he could stand this stupid camp long enough to wear these new clothes—and maybe earn those boots and the hat on the table that he figured were his size, since this know-it-all camp director seemed to have his number.

And Annie was here, a totally unexpected boon. While he was earning his points from Claire, maybe he could get a little something from Annie, too. There ought to be plenty of opportunity to catch her alone—in the barn, in the woods, in the meadow. His mind raced with the heady anticipation of getting in Annie's pants. So much so that he would embarrass himself if he had to get up right now. He tried to concentrate on Claire's closing remarks, but found his imagination going off on her, too. She looked hot, too, even if she was a lot older. Just meant more experience. Micah squirmed on the bench.

He glanced around and saw Seth's eyes narrowed on him, which cooled his libido faster than having a bucket of cold water thrown on him.

Damn, was the guy a mind reader? He didn't like this new authority figure in his life. Even Mr. Nester would have been better. Micah knew ole Nester inside and out, but this Seth guy? Micah hadn't figured him out yet—but he would.

He sure would.

CHAPTER ELEVEN

CLAIRE LET THE KIDS choose their daily chores from the list. Then she set them to the task of interviewing each other using a set of predetermined questions so that they could get to know one another better while she made a chart and timetable for their chores.

Through the open windows of the dining room she saw a big, dually truck and horse trailer pull into the parking area of the adjacent stable yard. Seth, who had been sitting close enough to Micah to keep him in line, looked out, then left the table.

"It's my brother Lane with Rube," he told her as he headed outside.

The driver circled, positioning the rig so that the trailer opened onto the barn area. Seth stopped abruptly in the doorway as the truck came to a stop with the cab facing their direction.

"What is *he* doing here?" he muttered.

"Something wrong?" Claire asked.

"No," Seth said, but the anger in his voice and his clenched fists told her otherwise.

She joined him at the door, following his gaze to an older man sitting in the passenger seat of the truck. "Who is that?"

"My loving father," he growled. "I'll be back in a few minutes."

A man wearing a big white Stetson stepped down from the driver's seat and came around the front of the cab. Even from a distance, Claire could see his resemblance to Seth, though he was stockier and had dark hair showing below his hat.

Curious about what was going on outside, Claire turned to her campers and said, "When you finish your interviews, I'll introduce you to your horses."

The brothers met halfway to the bunkhouse and shook hands, then Lane pulled Seth into a quick embrace and clapped him on the back a few times before Seth pulled away. Seth glared past his brother to the truck.

"I told you not to bring him," Seth said.

"What was I supposed to do? It's Dad. And I needed *his* truck and *his* trailer to get your horse up here."

Claire stepped onto the porch and the two men cut the conversation short. Clearly upset, Seth glanced from her to the man in the truck and back, then brought his brother over.

"Claire, this is my brother Lane. Claire's the director of the camp I told you about."

Lane's face broke into a broad grin that deepened the creases at the corners of his dark eyes. "So *you're* the one who wrangled my brother into real work? First person who's ever been able to do that."

Claire smiled. Lane was a nice-looking guy, but nothing to compare with his brooding younger brother. "I don't think it'll be nearly exciting enough for him, but he's stuck for a few weeks."

"There's not much that's as exciting as what he likes to do. But none of us ever talked any sense into him."

"Okay, enough," Seth said impatiently. "Help me get Rube out, so you can be on your way."

"Nice to meet you, Claire. If my baby brother gives you any trouble, just let me know. I can straighten him out—temporarily anyway." Lane tipped his hat, the grin diminishing as he headed toward the back of the trailer with Seth, who was obviously chewing him out.

Claire noticed the man in the truck watching his sons in disappointment. The truck windows were open and Claire wondered if he could hear their conversation. She followed far enough to watch them unload the horse.

Seth lowered the gate and spoke to the animal inside.

"Remember me, Rube?"

Rube answered with an immediate nicker and tried to turn his head toward Seth.

"Here, I'll get him," Lane said, then bounded up the ramp before Seth could answer. Lane brought out the horse. The gelding's light coat glistened, and although he was a little round from being retired to pasture, he looked sound and fit. His front legs displayed the typical dark inverted-V stocking pattern of a true roan and his mane, tail and face were a dark sorrel color. Intelligent brown eyes surveyed the new surroundings.

Drawn as always to a new horse, Claire joined them. "He's beautiful, Seth."

"He's a good fellow. Always has been. He'll enjoy having something to do this summer."

Claire spoke gently to Rube and the horse responded with a twitch of the ears and pushed his muzzle into her hand. There was an instant and palpable rapport between them and she knew she was going to fall in love with this horse—even as she struggled not to fall for his owner.

"You want me to saddle him real quick? Make sure he's going to work out?" Lane asked.

Seth hesitated. "I don't think—"

"Look, you might as well find out while I'm here to take him home," Lane insisted. "No need to disrupt his life, if he's not going to stay."

Claire waited for Seth's response, realizing that he might not be willing to admit to his brother that he needed a mounting block. As for wearing a helmet? Claire couldn't force him to wear a helmet with his own horse, so she wasn't going to say anything, even though he would be setting a bad example for the campers.

Finally Seth shrugged reluctantly.

Lane saddled Rube quickly and held on to the bridle.

"I'm going to mount on the offside," Seth said. "I still don't have enough strength in the bad leg yet."

"Not a problem," Lane said.

Rodeo and ranch horses were usually trained to accept a mount from either side. Even Claire's lesson horses were trained that way, but Seth hadn't asked and she hadn't thought to suggest it.

Rube never moved as Seth stuck his boot in the stirrup and pulled himself up to balance on the saddle with braced arms. Claire held her breath as Seth gingerly lifted his injured leg. Now came the tricky part—getting that leg over the saddle. A grimace shot across his face as he raised the leg higher, slowly making progress until he cleared the cantle. Claire let out a sigh of relief as he eased down in the saddle. She knew his ego had taken a bruising the past week from having to use the mounting block and wear her mandatory helmet. And he *would* have to wear that helmet on trail rides, even if he rode Rube. Camp policy for everybody.

As horse and rider walked away, she watched Seth's easy sway in perfect rhythm with Rube's long stride. The sounds of the truck door closing caught her attention.

"This is my father, Judd Morgan," Lane said as the older man joined them.

Judd tipped his hat to her. "Ma'am."

"Nice to meet you," Claire said, studying the rugged face for a moment and noticing that his eyes were the same golden color as Seth's. His hair was graying, but had once been the same as Seth's, as well. She wondered what had happened between them that had made Seth so angry to see him.

"He's looking a lot better than I expected, judging from when he was in the hospital," Judd said to Lane as Seth made a slow circle of the stable yard.

Seth nudged Rube into a slow trot, something he'd never done with Belle. Not too far, not for long, but an action that told Claire he felt comfortable on this horse.

He turned back to them and stopped a few feet away, as if reluctant to come closer. Father and son stared at each other in silence. Rube crab-stepped, his tail swishing, a sure sign that he was sensing Seth's tension. Seth pulled that black hat lower over his eyes and corrected the horse with the reins until Rube settled.

Judd broke the nerve-racking silence. "Just wanted to see that you were still alive."

"Libby could have told you that," Seth shot back.

"Wanted to see for myself."

"Now you've seen."

Claire listened in surprise to the open animosity between them. What was going on here?

"Yeah," Judd said flatly, "Seen and heard all I need to." He went back to the truck and climbed in, slamming the door behind him.

Sitting stiff and unmoving atop the horse. Seth could have been carved from stone, but the stricken look in his eyes told Claire he wasn't as unemotional as he pretended.

Lane closed the tailgate of the trailer, then came back to his brother.

"Look, Seth," Lane said in a low voice that Claire could barely hear. "Dad really wants to straighten things out. You could at least try."

"Yeah? Well, didn't sound that way to me. Tell him he can forget it." Seth's voice was angry and defensive. "I told you not to bring him."

"You are one stubborn-assed kid, Seth. You'd better get your head on straight before it's too late. One day you might regret you didn't take the first step, no matter who's at fault."

Seth shifted in the saddle and stared into the distance but didn't respond. Lane glowered up at him for a minute, then joined their father in the truck. The rig pulled away and Claire took hold of Rube's bridle.

"Do you want to go to the block to dismount?" she asked.

"I can get down," he snapped.

Claire bristled. "I don't know what just went on here between you and your father, but don't think for a minute you can bring that attitude to my camp."

Seth's chest heaved, but he held his tongue and eased off the horse. He took the reins from her without a word and limped off toward the barn leading Rube. Claire started after him, but the campers trailed out of the dining room and she had to turn her attention to them.

· · · ·

LATE THAT NIGHT, after lights-out, Claire and Seth sat at a table in the dining room, rehashing the day and scheduling the chores for tomorrow. Seth was having a problem concentrating with Claire so close, yet so inaccessible. Her hands-off attitude had preyed on his mind all day in addition to the ugly scene with his father. At least she hadn't brought that up—yet. She was being absolutely professional—and it was driving him insane, because right now, professional was the last thing he'd wanted to be around her.

"The kids did a good job divvying the chores among themselves," Claire said, studying the sign-up sheet. She turned it around for Seth to see.

He laid a finger on an entry, trying to ignore her hand so close to his. "Not good."

"What?" She leaned closer to see what he was pointing at.

"Micah signed up for the same chores as Annie," he said.

"That's no problem. There's plenty of work to go around, feeding the livestock."

"I'm not worried about that. I'm worried about Micah around Annie. He's got the hots for her."

"How do you know that? He's only been here a few hours."

Seth pursed his lips, recalling the look on Micah's face as he'd stared at the girl. "Trust me, Claire, I know when a guy's craving a woman."

She glanced up at him, her lips parted slightly, and he couldn't help himself; he leaned over to kiss her.

"Seth, no," she said, drawing away. "We need to talk about Micah and Annie. Why do you think there's a problem?"

Frustrated and disappointed, Seth sat back, staring at the two names side by side on the paper. "I know what I'm talking about. If Annie starts acting funny, you might want to separate them."

Claire scribbled in her notebook. "Okay, I've jotted it down. I hope it doesn't come to that, but I don't want to take choices away from them so soon. Let's give him a chance."

"Whatever you say. But I'm duct-taping him in."

"What?" Claire said. "I don't understand."

"Old trick of my daddy's when I used to slip out at night after Lane had gone off to college. Dad laid a strip of duct tape on my door, from the doorknob across the jamb. If I opened the door, I couldn't restick the tape, and he knew."

"What if you had to go to the bathroom in the middle of the night?"

"No excuse. My bedroom had its own bathroom. I was pretty much stuck."

Claire pursed her lips, studying his face. "Somehow I find it hard to believe that stopped you."

Seth grinned. "Well, it all depended on how bad I wanted out. And, darlin', if I want something bad enough, nothing's going to stop me."

Claire cleared her throat. "Some things you can't have, no matter how much you want them."

"Oh? Like us?"

She hesitated, then nodded slightly. "Like us."

"I'm not done yet," Seth said. "So don't get that set in your head."

"You *are* done, so get that out of *your* head." Claire pulled the chore chart back to her side of the table. "Did Micah give you any trouble when you picked him up yesterday?"

"No, not really. Just a little attitude."

"You ought to be able to identify with that."

Seth pictured the squalid trailer, the disheveled mother and Micah's embarrassment. The look in the woman's eyes haunted him.

"Something else on your mind?" Claire asked.

"I don't know if I should mention it. Probably nothing can be done, anyway."

"What? About Micah?"

"Maybe it's none of our business, Claire, but his living conditions are not good at all. Have you ever been there?"

"No, I worked through the high school counselor on everything. I did interview Micah and his mother at the school, but I had no authority to do a home visit." She frowned. "Tell me what you saw."

"I think his mother needs help as much or more than he does. She's just...lost, I think. Micah said she went into a tailspin after his dad went to prison. She looked groggy, too, like maybe she's on something. And I'm wondering, what if he does get something good out of camp? He still has to go back home afterward."

"Good point," Claire said as she jotted more notes on her pad. "I'll make some discreet inquiries to see if there's some way to help her. Thanks for telling me, Seth. It helps Micah, too."

Seth thought about that. "I don't know that I've helped him. I didn't know exactly what to say when he was talking, so I mostly listened. When it comes to advising these kids, I'm not on the same level with your other assistant."

Claire tilted her head slightly as she tamped the stack of papers together into a neat rectangle. "Yes, but he quit, so he's of no help at all, is he? At least you're here and listening."

Seth shrugged. He hoped it would be that simple.

"I think the new clothes were a good idea," Claire said, moving on. "Everybody seemed pretty excited about them."

"Micah was, for sure."

"He just seemed angry that he had to give in and take them."

"He was trying his best to hide it, but trust me, if he'd been a girl, you'd have heard some shrieking. His clothes are worn-out, and from the looks of that trailer, he didn't have much hope of anything better."

"That breaks my heart. You really learned a lot about him in a short time. I'm impressed."

"I'm glad something about me impresses you." Seth leaned toward her once more, hoping against hope she'd let him kiss her this time.

No dice. She drew away, out of range. Seth eased back in his seat. *No fair, Claire.*

Seth was tired and his mind unsettled after the confrontation with his father—certainly not in the mood for games. He rose and picked up his hat from the table.

"Is that all for today?"

"Are you okay?" she asked. "I mean, do you want to talk about your father?"

Seth frowned. That was the *last* thing he wanted to talk about. Especially with her.

"It's my problem. Nothing you can do about it."

She shrugged slightly. "Sometimes just talking can—"

"You don't want to talk about why we can't be together and I don't want to talk about my family problems. So we're even. Anything else tonight?"

"Nope, don't need you for a thing," Claire said sharply. "Good night."

"Figures," Seth muttered, plopping his hat on his head as he headed out the door.

CHAPTER TWELVE

CLAIRE SPENT A RESTLESS night filled with dreams of Seth. Finally she gave up on sleep and lay awake, staring into the darkness, listening to the soft breathing of the girls in the next room, trying to make sense of her conflicting emotions.

At the first hint of dawn, she pushed the covers off and sat up in bed, staring at the opposite wall. A long-term relationship with Seth was out of the question.

Right?

Of course. So why couldn't she convince herself?

Maybe because of the desire rising in her, just thinking about the possibility. Or the blaze that had licked at her insides when he'd tried to kiss her. Then again, would enjoying his kisses or appreciating his out-and-out sex appeal mean she had to fall in love with him? They could part at the close of camp and that would be end of it, right?

Face it, Claire, you just flat-out want him. Recipe for disaster, she admonished herself sternly. Time for a cold shower and a reality check. The cold shower was invigorating, the reality check not as successful. Claire tried to organize her camp plans as she dressed.

Yesterday's unstructured afternoon had allowed the teenagers to get to know their horses, then ample free time to wind down and do their own thing, within reason. But on Monday morning chores started right after breakfast. Claire planned to continue Seth's therapy while the campers were helping the ranch hands—if Seth still wanted to, now that he had Rube to ride. She stepped outside and knocked on his door to make sure he had the boys up in time for breakfast.

He opened the door, barefoot and bare chested, wearing sweatpants that hugged his hipbones. He wiped his face with a towel. The sheen on his chest and the damp hair tousled over his forehead suggested he'd been exercising. Hard. Claire pressed her lips together to keep her mouth from going slack and tucked her hands into her back pockets to resist the urge to touch the smooth skin of that solid chest.

Meltdown time.

"I see you're up and ready to go."

Seth's mouth twitched into a devilish grin as he captured her gaze. "Anytime you are, darling."

She was growing accustomed to his teasing. "I'll let you know."

He lifted an eyebrow. "You do that."

"You'd better get the boys moving. Breakfast in an hour, then chores. I think that's a good time for your therapy rides, while they're busy, don't you?"

"Whatever you say, but I'm not wearing a helmet, since they're not going to be around."

Claire repeated her rule about helmets on trail rides. "Everybody, including you, has to wear one."

"Taking Rube out for therapy isn't technically a trail ride," he countered.

Claire huffed. "I'm not going to waste my time fighting as long as you're not on one of my horses. It's your own head you're risking anyway."

"Life's all about risks."

"True, but some risks can be avoided."

Seth cocked his head at her. "You take bigger risks than I do, Claire."

"Hardly."

He waved his arm toward the dorms. "Sure you do. This camp, for instance. You're risking these kids' emotional stability, your sponsors' money, your own reputation. And your riding school. What if one of your riders gets hurt?"

Claire drew herself up, offended. "I take all sorts of extra precautions with my riders—and my campers."

"Except with me. You really took a risk when you hired me, just on Libby's say-so."

"I had you checked out."

"You had my *background* checked out. But you have no idea how I'll affect these boys psychologically, especially Micah. Do you?"

Claire started to argue, then clamped her lips shut. He had a point. Finally she said, "I'm hoping for the best."

"Exactly. The same as I do when I climb on a bull's back."

"But you don't *have* to ride bulls."

"And you could have a normal riding school and spend the summers relaxing."

"No, I—"

"You couldn't. That's my point," Seth finished for her. "Because you need the challenge and you want to help others."

"True."

"And the risks are worth it."

She chewed on her lower lip. She hadn't thought about her choices in that way before. "But, Seth, you could easily be killed. I don't risk my life or my kids' lives."

"Okay, I'll give you that, but I'm willing to take the risk, just like you are. Claire, I want to know you better. At least give me the chance." He lifted her chin and gave her an endearing smile. "I'd be worth it, I promise."

Claire pulled away uneasily. He had no idea how close she was to giving in. "Get dressed so we can set up the dining room before Rosie brings breakfast."

Seth sighed in resignation. "Sure."

· · · ·

AFTER BREAKFAST AND CHORES, work began with the campers and their horses as a group, teaching them the basics: catching the horse, haltering, leading, saddling and bridling, grooming and equipment care. Seth worked with the boys while she taught the girls. Mary Lou loved horses and had been around them quite a bit, so she picked everything up quickly. Annie didn't have experience with horses, but she'd always wanted one, so she was eager to learn.

Seth wasn't so lucky. Claire could overhear Micah giving him grief about having to follow instructions, and Jason was afraid of animals. A chill ran across Claire's shoulders as snippets of remembered conversation between her father and Cody flickered through her mind.

You will brand that calf.

Dad, don't make me. I hate it.

You're gonna have to get over being afraid of the livestock, son. You're a ranch kid. You've got to pull your weight. Do it!

Please, Dad, I can't. I can't...I can't...

"You can do it. Go ahead."

Claire jerked around, her heart racing, and headed toward Seth and the boys. She wasn't going to have her campers intimidated or frightened.

But the voice she'd heard wasn't her father's. Trying to slow her breathing, she stopped a few feet away to see how Seth handled the situation before she intervened.

He gave her a puzzled look. "What's wrong?"

"Nothing...nothing. Just observing."

He clenched his jaw, but turned back to Jason, who held a hoof pick in his hand and stared at his horse's foot as if it were a snake about to strike.

"Face the rear and stand next to his shoulder." Seth took Jason by the arm and guided him into place. "Now run your hand down his leg and give a slight squeeze just above the fetlock."

Jason looked up at him in bewilderment.

"The fetlock is like the ankle, right above his hoof. He'll lift his foot for you, I promise." Seth pointed to the spot.

Hesitantly Jason slid his hand down the leg and squeezed. The horse lifted his foot. Jason jumped, but gamely held on. Seth showed him how to use a hoof pick to rake any debris from the crevices of the foot and then turn the tool over to use the brush side to remove any loose dirt.

"Ease the foot down—don't drop it."

Jason beamed as he lowered the hoof and looked to Seth for approval.

"Good job. Now the back hoof." Seth glanced toward Micah. "Are you paying attention? You're next."

Micah pretended to be unconcerned, but he had been watching closely until Seth looked at him. Smart kid, but stubborn. Claire breathed easier and went back to her girls, satisfied with Seth's instruction. She overheard Micah's raised voice another time or two, but he apparently got the job done and all the horses were turned out to pasture a few minutes later.

When they returned to the dorm, the teenagers preceded Claire and Seth, giving the adults a moment to speak.

"How do you think the first day went?" Claire asked.

"No big problems."

"What about Micah? I heard him giving you a bit of trouble."

"Micah's being Micah. He's trying to look cool by being tough. He'll get over it. Let's see, what's next on the agenda? A hike this afternoon and free time before dinner?"

"Very good," Claire said, pleased. The hike would be across the valley since Seth's leg wasn't ready for the steep incline of mountain trails. "You're right on top of things."

Seth grinned that crooked grin and caught her by the arms, turning her to face him. "I always am. Remember that."

"Seth!" Claire pulled back, then caught a movement from the corner of her eye. The campers stood on the porch watching them with interest.

Seth glared at their audience. "Aren't you guys supposed to be getting your gear together for the hike? Go to it."

When the kids disappeared inside, Seth turned back to Claire and stroked his fingers down her cheek. The undisguised hunger in his eyes touched off an answering longing in her. All she had to do was say the word and she'd be back in his arms.

Instead, she jerked away.

"Don't try that again as long as this camp is in session. Ever!"

• • • •

A FTER THE HIKE, refreshing showers and a filling dinner, Seth gathered with the others in the dining room, curious to see what Claire had in mind. She set a large pad of paper on an easel at the front of the room. Seth took a seat at a table behind the kids as she picked up a red marker.

"Tonight we're going to talk about self-esteem. Who knows the difference between self-esteem and conceit?"

At first the teens sat silent, looking neither at her nor one another.

"Anybody want to hazard a guess?" Claire said patiently. "Can a person have high self-esteem without being conceited?"

Micah propped one foot on the bench seat and laid his arm across his knee. "No, they're the same thing," he said. "Just means you think you're better than the next guy."

"No, it doesn't," Mary Lou said. "Self-esteem means you feel good about yourself, no matter what."

"And what if you don't have anything to feel good about?" Micah retorted.

"Then you find something," Mary Lou said.

Before long all four teenagers were engrossed in the conversation, with Claire moderating whenever the discussion threatened to turn to argument. When one of the campers made a good point, she would write it on the pad in either the "Self-Esteem" or "Conceit" column.

Then she flipped to a clean sheet of paper and wrote, "How We Let the Feathers Out of Our Pillow."

What? Seth noticed the teens sit up straighter, waiting with rapt interest for her to explain that. He leaned forward, too, completely into the game now.

She pulled a pillow from behind the easel and plumped it. "This pillow is like your self-esteem holder. It's filled to the brim with self-esteem when you're born. Then..."

With a pair of manicure scissors, she snipped a tiny hole in the covering. "Then, maybe without even meaning to, somebody gives you a little cut."

She plumped the pillow again.

"Do you see what happens?"

Feathers drifted out.

"That's your self-esteem leaking out." She snipped again, then again. "Each time you're put down, whether by somebody else or by yourself, you lose more self-esteem."

She snipped more holes.

"If this happens enough over the years, your fluffy pillow of self-esteem goes flat. So let's make a list of things we say or do to others or to ourselves to flatten that pillow."

Micah refused to participate, but the others called out answers faster than Claire could write them. Seth went to the front of the room and grabbed another marker to help her get all the responses down. She graced him with a radiant smile that made him more determined than ever to win her over in spite of the dilemma constantly playing out in his head. If he fell in love with her and she hated bull riding, would he give it up? And what did he have to offer her, anyway?

Not ready to admit he was indeed falling in love, and unwilling to accept that he might never ride bulls again, Seth had no idea what to do. He needed to find out why she was so averse to any type of rodeo, and then maybe he could convince her to let him into her life long enough to test the waters. Right now, their relationship was not even a one-night stand, and for once that really bothered him.

"Okay, okay, I think we've got enough." Claire laid her marker in the tray and Seth did the same.

"We're going to hang this sheet on the bulletin board, so it's there all the time to remind us what hurts. For tomorrow, be thinking what we can do to patch that pillow and refill it with feathers."

"Kill a chicken," Micah offered. "There are plenty around here."

"Shut *up*, Micah," Mary Lou said. "If that's the only thing you've got to say, nobody wants to hear it."

He gave an exaggerated grimace. "Aww, now you've poked another hole in my little pillow and all my feathers are coming out."

Mary Lou's face fell. "I did, didn't I?" she said seriously. "I'm sorry."

Micah was thrown off balance for an instant. "I...that's oka—" Then he caught himself. "Hey, nothing you can say bothers me. I don't have any stupid pillow to worry about."

"Let's get to bed," Claire interjected. "Long day tomorrow. Up at six for breakfast and out for chores by seven."

· · · ·

A collective groan went up, but they ambled onto the porch and into their separate rooms. Claire ripped the two large sheets of paper from the pad and had Seth hang them on the bulletin board near the door, while she swept up the elusive feathers scattered across the floor. The group's eager participation had made the mess worthwhile.

She reached back when something tickled her neck. Seth chuckled softly, and she twisted around to catch him with a feather in his hand. He grinned and dropped it onto the pile at her feet, then stooped to hold the dustpan while she swept.

Just when she had the feathers corralled, Seth blew them out of the pan, sending them flying. She frowned at him, but he cocked his head to one side and deepened his grin.

"Seth!" she declared, dropping to her knees to scoop the feathers back into the dustpan. "If you keep that up, we'll be here all night."

He waggled an eyebrow. "Yep. Looks like the only way I can spend any time with you."

"Nooo! I still have things to do tonight before I go to sleep."

"I can think of things, too."

Their foreheads almost touched as Seth hovered over her. Claire tried to ignore him, but he leaned even closer, until he could kiss her if she turned her face up to him. Instead, she covered the dustpan with her hand so he couldn't blow the feathers off again.

"We're not going to do anything you can think of."

"We could talk."

"About what?"

"About why you won't give us a chance."

"There is no *us*." Claire stared at the feathers rather than look at him and give him an opening.

"There could be. And it would be a good thing."

She glanced at him in surprise. He wasn't smiling anymore but was dead serious. His breath fanned her lips, making it extremely hard to think rationally. It was a good thing he couldn't hear her heart pounding; he might think she actually wanted him to kiss her. Or more.

"Not here where the kids could walk in at any time."

"When?"

"I don't know. I...I have to give it some thought." Every time he got this close, Claire teetered on the brink of losing her resolve. She shook her head to clear it.

Somehow, she had to get it through his skull that there would be no relationship between them. And she had to convince herself, as well.

CHAPTER THIRTEEN

THE NEXT MORNING while Claire escorted the campers to their designated ranch hands to begin their chores, Seth saddled Rube and Jack. When she arrived, the two of them mounted and rode away from the barn, headed down a long narrow valley between towering mountain ranges. Being on a ranch again invigorated Seth. He'd always loved the outdoors, hunting and fishing, riding and hiking, and he was impatient for his leg to heal so he could get back to normal.

He'd worried a lot lately about when he could return to bull riding. What he hadn't allowed himself to think about was what he would do if he really couldn't compete in the only occupation he understood and did well.

Claire was putting him through an increasingly difficult regimen of exercises to condition and stretch his leg. Day by day he had noticed the improvement, but he hadn't lost the limp, and if he stepped wrong he had to struggle to keep his balance. What if...

He brought himself up short. No point even thinking like that yet.

"I did get in touch with somebody to look into helping Mrs. Abbott. Her name is Terri Harper and she volunteers her time to help women in need," Claire said. "Maybe Micah will go home to something better."

Seth tried to concentrate on her words as she talked about Micah's mother, but her lips and sparkling eyes distracted him. He nudged Rube closer until he and Claire rubbed knees. Catching Jack's rein, he brought both horses to a stop.

"What are you doing?" she asked.

"We're out here alone. No kids to walk in. Nobody to overhear. So tell me why you refuse to give me a chance."

She fiddled with Jack's mane, smoothing a stray lock into place above his withers.

"Claire?"

Finally, she met Seth's gaze. "I've given you the reason. Me, boss. You, employee. That's enough."

"But not the real reason. Look, if you truly can't stand me, just tell me why and I'll leave you alone."

A tiny smile quirked the corners of her mouth. "Really? That's all it would take?"

"If it's the truth."

"Well, then, here goes. You're arrogant, you've got a rotten attitude sometimes, you're going to be gone in a few weeks—and you're a bull rider."

"So, if I stop bull riding and take up calf roping, would that do it?"

"I told you, I don't like rodeo. I don't like anything about it."

"Because you consider it cruel?"

Claire hesitated. "That's part of it."

"Part of it? What's the rest?"

Tears clouded her eyes as she shook her head.

"Claire, tell me. I want to understand what I'm up against."

"I heard you working with Jason yesterday. The way he's afraid of horses reminds me a lot of my brother. Cody was afraid of animals all his life. He stuck out like a sore thumb in our family because we all loved and worked with them."

"That's tough, growing up on a ranch and being afraid of animals."

"More than you can imagine. Especially with Dad being the foreman and expecting both his kids to pull their weight around the ranch. Cody was a talented artist, a cartoonist. But Dad thought that was sissy, and he made Cody do ranch work. Even the branding and castrating. Cody would puke the whole time. It's good Dad never was physically abusive, because he got so angry at times I thought he'd hit Cody."

Seth listened, trying to imagine that sort of fear. The first time he'd ever felt anything close to it was the day he awoke in the hospital and the doctor had said he'd never ride again. Since then, he'd fought off panic attacks—but never out of fear of the animal that injured him, just of his own frailty.

Seth dismounted. "Let's walk," he said.

When Claire joined him on the ground, he took the reins of both horses in one hand and wrapped his other arm around her waist. She resisted at first, then gave in and leaned against him. Overhead, white clouds floated by, in sharp contrast to the cobalt sky. Birds called from the trees along the edge of the valley, and the horses' hooves swished through the lush meadow grasses as they walked.

"When Cody was a teenager, Dad taught him to rope, and made him enter the tie-down events at the high school rodeos. Cody hated it. He was afraid of breaking his fingers and not being able to draw. Dad wouldn't relent, even though Mom sided with my brother."

They walked in silence, arm in arm, for a while. Seth waited for her to continue.

"If you hate something, you're not good at it," Claire said softly, "and Cody was definitely not good at roping. His lack of competitiveness made Dad furious."

She looked up at Seth. "It's hard for you to understand, isn't it?"

"The part about being scared, yes. But I didn't do what my father expected, either, so I can relate to the angry-father bit." He paused, then said, "Go on, finish telling me about Cody."

"It's so hard to think about him...."

"This is the first time I've heard you mention him. I assume he died?"

"Yes, sadly. At sixteen. One night after a particularly bad go-round in Bozeman, Cody and Dad got into their usual scrap over his performance. Cody had come in last, and he was humiliated and upset when Dad told him any fool should improve a *little* over time. Dad let him take off for home in his truck. Usually Mom or I rode with Cody, but he left without us. We begged Dad to go after him and calm him down. He wouldn't, saying, 'Let him go. He's got to grow up sometime.'"

She shuddered and began sobbing quietly. "Cody didn't go home. Maybe he was running away or just driving around to cool off. We'll never know. But somewhere on the other side of Bozeman, headed away from home, he lost control of his truck and hit a tree. Or hit a tree deliberately...."

Seth dropped the reins to ground-tie the horses. He drew Claire close to his chest, stroking her hair to soothe her. She eased away enough to wipe her eyes with her palms.

"I'm sorry, I shouldn't have unloaded on you."

"No, I needed to know."

"Seth, don't insist there's something between us. I meant what I said. I'm not going to get involved with a rider."

"What about a *former* rider?"

"I heard you talking to Dad. You're going back as soon as you can."

"The doctor says I might never ride another bull, Claire."

"He said *might* not. What if your leg heals to the point you can? You know you'll go back."

"Not if I say I won't."

Claire looked up at him in bewilderment. "Seth, you told me not being able to ride would be like cutting out your heart. How could I possibly expect you to do that?"

"Claire..."

"No, listen to me. I know what riding means to you. I see the passion in your eyes when you talk about it. You love it. And you don't know if you'll ever love me. Suppose—"

Seth interrupted her before she could go on. "I do know. Trust me, I know exactly how I feel about you. I wouldn't be talking like this if I didn't."

Claire held his face in her hands. "Then I would be asking you to choose between your two loves. And how could either of us be sure you made the right choice?"

"I won't make a decision I can't live with," he said.

Claire shook her head doubtfully. "I appreciate the offer, but it's far too early to make that kind of promise." She searched his eyes as if gauging his sincerity. "You think about what you're saying, Seth. Would it be worth the sacrifice?"

As he held her in his arms, wanting her to be his so much he ached inside, Seth's thoughts raced. *Could* he live with the decision never to ride again? And would he have anything worthwhile to offer Claire if he didn't? Was getting on another bull the only way for him to feel complete? That was the question he needed to answer.

Claire was different from any woman he'd ever met. Kind, intelligent, nurturing, always concerned about people less fortunate. Every time he saw her, touched her, he knew he'd give up almost anything to have her love. He'd never fallen this hard for anyone, not even his first head-over-heels infatuation back in high school, a girl who'd devastated him by leaving him for a geek who could help her with her algebra.

Then he had an alarming notion—might Claire be drawn to him because he was injured and needed fixing? Would she feel the same after he healed?

An even bigger question was how *he* would feel if he couldn't prove to himself, or to Claire, that he was whole again.

Pushing negative thoughts aside, Seth nuzzled her cheek, then kissed her, their lips parting, touching again, opening, accepting, exploring.

Her fingers toyed with the hair at the nape of his neck and she pulled him into a deeper kiss, eliciting a low moan from him. Their individual scents, rising with the increasing body heat being generated between them, blended into a potent aphrodisiac.

"You're driving me crazy," he murmured between kisses.

She buried her face in his neck, breathless. "Seth...I didn't expect this...to feel this way about you. What if it doesn't work out?"

He lifted her chin with his fingertips. "We'll never know if we don't try."

Thoroughly aroused, Seth trailed his lips along her cheek, down her neck, drawn to the soft curve of her breasts. She caught his face in her hands and lifted it away from her body.

"We have to go back. Chore time is almost over."

"Come on, Claire," Seth groaned. "Not yet." He grasped her hands, kissing each palm in turn. "Those kids can wait another few minutes."

"No, we can't be late."

She gently withdrew his hands and moved away from him, leaving him longing for more. "Besides, I have to think about all this—and so do you."

. . . .

THAT AFTERNOON, Claire began groundwork with the horses and campers. Each student had twenty minutes to accomplish the assignment for the day. If they didn't succeed, they would have to leave the pen and work on the same task the next day. The time limit took into account the horses' welfare as well as the teens' attention span, to avoid a situation where they became frustrated and began to act out. If success came before the allotted time was up, the pair was allowed to leave the pen, their work done for the day.

The first day's assignment was easy enough. Get the horse to walk, trot and stop on voice command. Claire was confident the animals understood the commands but knew they would test the kids every step of the way. The students could use a lunge whip to urge the horses on but could not touch or frighten them with it.

Claire demonstrated what she expected with Belle, showing how to hold the lunge whip pointed toward the horse's hip to encourage it to go forward, and then just ahead of the horse on the stop command. She put Belle through her paces, including more difficult maneuvers that the campers would be expected to master before the summer ended. A murmur of doubt ran through the group.

"You can do it. All of you. Wait and see. Mary Lou, why don't you go first?"

Horse lover that she was, the girl had her horse responding within ten minutes. The animal was rewarded with encouraging pats and they left the ring. Jason and Annie took longer during their turns, but both found ways to convince the horses to respond.

Micah went last, leading a tall dun horse that the cowboys called Monkey Business, because he was always up to some trick or other. He wasn't a mean-spirited horse, just a prankster, but Claire felt Micah needed the challenge.

The horse shied going through the gate, dragging Micah a few steps until he regained control. When the teen unsnapped the lead rope, Monkey Business bolted to the side of the round pen, turning to glance at him with a look that seemed to say, "So there!"

Micah glared back at the horse as he picked up the lunge whip from the center of the arena.

"Remember what I told you, Micah," Claire said from her perch atop the fence, where she could easily intervene if necessary. "Take a deep breath to calm yourself before you ask him to do anything."

From the set of Micah's jaw and his grimly pressed lips, it wasn't working.

"Ask him to walk, Micah. Point the whip toward his flank," she instructed.

Seth moved beside Claire, climbing up and straddling the fence. "The horse is a little spooked," he murmured. "Maybe you should give Micah another one."

"Let's at least give him a chance before I pull him out."

"Whatever you say."

"Walk," Micah said.

Monkey Business lifted a lip in defiance, but not a single hoof.

Micah flicked the whip and commanded, "Walk, you stupid animal."

The horse shook his mane as if he understood, but still didn't move. When Micah stomped his foot, Monkey shied away and put his nose over the top rail, whinnying at the horses outside the pen, clearly making a monkey out of Micah. Obviously unhappy, the teen popped the whip hard and shouted, "Walk, I said!"

"All right, that's enough, Micah. Out of the pen." Claire hopped down and opened the gate.

Micah shot a killing look at her then the horse. As he strode out the gate, he said, "Nobody could make that horse do anything."

"Do you want me to show you?" she asked.

"No," Micah said with a sneer. "You're a trainer. Of course, you can make him move. Bet nobody else could, though." He looked defiantly at Seth. "Bet *he* couldn't."

Seth, male that he was, took up the challenge without a word and without Claire's sanction. He limped into the round pen, where Monkey was happily swishing his tail in triumph and calling to the other horses.

Claire caught him by the arm as he passed her. "Seth, you don't have to prove anything. I'll give Micah another horse tomorrow, like you suggested."

"Too late now. He has to finish what he started. The horse, too," Seth said, never taking his eyes off Monkey. "Come here, Micah, and stand beside me."

Reluctantly, the teen obeyed. Monkey had the two of them in his sights now. He snorted when Seth stopped a few feet away and spoke in a low voice, not a command, just talking the way he would to a person. After a minute Monkey lowered his head, his ears relaxed and twitching back and forth.

"Good boy," Seth said. "Good boy."

He reached slowly for the lunge whip. The horse pricked his ears sharply forward, his eyes moving from the whip to Seth and back. Seth raised it slightly. "Walk," he said firmly.

The horse gave Seth a defiant look.

"Walk." Seth raised the whip another few inches and took a step that put him more to the animal's rear.

Monkey snorted loudly, shook his mane hard, then took a step forward, then another. The campers cheered. The horse tossed his head in irritation, but Seth bobbled the end of the whip and he kept walking.

"Trot," Seth commanded.

Monkey seemed to give it a moment's thought, then broke into a slow, plodding trot.

After a few strides, Seth called, "Walk."

Monkey obeyed.

Seth took a step forward and pointed the whip at Monkey's chest. "Whoa."

The horse stopped.

"Good boy," Seth crooned. "Good Monkey." He laid the whip down and slowly approached the animal. When he reached the gelding's side, he patted his neck firmly, continuing the praise. Monkey shoved his muzzle into his hand.

"Your turn, Micah," Seth said, going back to the center of the ring.

"He won't do that for me," the boy protested.

"We'll see. Pick up the whip."

Micah finally got the horse to respond to a couple of commands, and Claire allowed him to end the lesson, but nobody was fooled. Monkey's obedience was due to Seth's presence in the pen. Claire had a good idea what tomorrow would bring, with Micah in there alone.

Seth snapped the lead rope on Monkey's halter and handed it to the boy.

"Spend a little more time with him, get to know him. He's a lot like you."

"No way! Stubborn son of a—"

Seth frowned at Micah and the boy stopped short. He led the horse away and turned him out to pasture with the others.

"I don't think he gets it," Seth said to Claire, fastening the gate to the round pen.

"I'm sure he doesn't. Not yet, anyway."

"I'll see that he does."

"Seth...remember, we're here to help him."

"Exactly what I intend to do."

• • • •

THE NEXT FEW DAYS PASSED quickly. Claire kept the hours filled with activities, yet gave the campers ample leisure time, as well. Seth circumvented any ideas Micah might have had about sneaking out of the dorm by telling him about the duct-taped door. The only other way out was through Seth's room, and so far Micah had not tested Seth's claim to be a light sleeper. He did, however, walk a fine line between not doing anything bad enough to be punished, yet finding a way to irritate Seth daily. So far Seth hadn't docked Micah any points, but if the time came, Claire intended to back him fully.

The teenagers seemed to benefit from the daily self-esteem and mutual-trust discussions, role-playing sessions and outdoor activities that fostered cooperation as well as self-reliance. The groundwork with the horses was progressing—except for Micah, who lagged a couple of days behind the others. Claire had offered him another horse, but Micah had a point to prove with Monkey Business and he refused. For the daily trail rides, however, she infuriated the teen by giving him a gentle, plodding horse.

"I can ride Monkey," he insisted. "I don't need a plow horse."

"Not until you can handle him in the pen," Claire said.

"If I could pop him with that whip once or twice, he'd mind," Micah grumbled.

"You need to earn his respect, Micah, not his fear."

"Fear, respect.... What's the difference?"

"I think when you figure that out, you'll find Monkey's no trouble at all."

And so Micah rode the gentle plodder, grumbling more each day when he garnered no progress with Monkey in the pen. He resented any advice, especially Seth's, and even Claire was growing impatient with him.

As the days passed, Claire and Seth got to know one another better. His behavior in public was totally professional, but whenever he got her to himself, he made his desires clear. Wonderfully, deliciously clear.

Their morning therapy rides consisted of flexing and conditioning Seth's leg on the way out, more flexing on the way back—and stealing kisses. Claire had nixed any expectation of sex until camp ended, taking no chance of being accused of inappropriate behavior with minors around.

One morning, during their ride, Seth asked, "Do you miss your mother? You rarely mention her."

"Of course, I do. But we talk almost every day. She's so busy giving horse-gentling seminars and doing private horse therapy that we wouldn't have much time together anyway. I'm really proud of her and happy that she's doing what she loves."

"That's good to know. It means a lot to love what you do," Seth said wistfully, and Claire knew he was thinking about bull riding. They hadn't talked again about his offer to give it up, and she was reluctant to mention it herself.

"I wish my dad understood that," he added.

Finally, an opening to get him to talk about his father. Claire didn't let it pass. "What happened between you? I got the feeling this rift isn't new."

Seth shook his head. "No, it's been going on awhile. He wanted me to go to college—he saved the money for all of us to go. But I rebelled. I'd had more than enough of school. Not only didn't I go to college, but I left home against his wishes and joined the bull riding circuit."

Seth fell silent and Claire didn't press him. Finally he pulled Rube to a stop on a knoll. He stared across the valley below for a long time before finally continuing.

"I thought I was going to blow the top off the bull riding world and strut back home to flaunt it in my father's face. I came pretty close, too." Bitter disappointment rang in Seth's voice. "Instead I wound up just like he said I would, broken up with nothing to fall back on. And he's the one who gets to gloat."

"I didn't see him gloating the other day, Seth. I saw a father who didn't know how to reach his son."

"You heard what he said."

"Yes, but I also saw two men so much alike that neither one could compromise."

"You sound like Lane," Seth said, and Claire could hear the aggravation in his tone.

"Maybe we're both right."

"Or maybe you're wrong." Seth reined Rube around and headed for home.

After that, Seth rarely mentioned bull riding, even to her father, although one day he'd driven into Bozeman for X-rays that were sent to the Dallas surgeon who had operated on his leg.

When he returned from Bozeman, Seth hadn't shared the prognosis, so she asked him.

He'd shrugged her off. "It'll be a few days before I hear from Doc. Doesn't matter."

She still didn't know what the surgeon had said.

But Claire couldn't think about that today. Natalie was due for a lesson in an hour. Seth had taken the boys on a hike, and the girls wanted to learn to be side-walkers, so Claire had agreed to allow them to help the Rider girls, as volunteers.

By the time Natalie arrived, Annie and Mary Lou knew their duties. Natalie, in good spirits as usual, was delighted to meet the campers and have them participate.

When she was in the saddle on Belle, she looked around from her perch. "Where's Seth?" she asked.

"On a hike," Claire told her.

"I wanted to see him," Natalie said with a pout. She had grown accustomed to his attendance at her lessons.

"Maybe he'll be back before you finish. Now, let's get started."

For the next half hour Natalie went through the motions of the lesson, but her eyes constantly scanned the fence line. Claire repeatedly reminded her to pay attention. On one round, Natalie waved to her mother, who watched from a folding chair just inside the paddock gate. On the next round, the girl waved again, with great vigor.

"Hey, Seth!" she cried.

"Hey, girl!" Seth replied, stepping up on one of the lower boards of the fence to hang his arms over the top. "You're looking good up there."

Natalie beamed. "Come ride with me, okay, Seth? You promised you would one day."

Claire cocked her head at him. After all his finagling to get out of wearing a helmet, he was sure to refuse.

Seth made a face, pretending disappointment. "By the time I get a horse saddled, your lesson will be over."

Exactly what Claire had expected.

"I don't mind waiting," Natalie said hopefully, looking back at him as Belle was led away.

"Natalie, keep your eyes on Belle's ears so you don't lose your balance," Claire called.

Micah climbed onto the fence beside Seth. When he saw tiny Natalie on huge Belle, with the volunteers walking beside her, he pointed and snickered.

Claire saw Seth glare at Micah, although she couldn't hear what he said. Whatever it was, Micah closed his mouth, though his expression hadn't changed.

The next time she looked, Seth was gone, but Micah was still there, and still scowling. She wasn't going to wait for Seth to dock him points—she would do it herself tonight. About that time, Seth reappeared, leading Rube, saddled and haltered. He led the horse into the arena.

"Seth, you *are* going to ride!" Natalie exclaimed.

"Guess I can saddle up faster than I thought," Seth said, adjusting the girth and lowering the stirrup.

"Is that your horse? He's so pretty."

"Yep, this is Rube."

Claire was not amused. Seth was going to break her helmet rule and she'd have to make some explanation to Natalie. Then she realized he didn't have his hat on and a helmet hung by the strap on the pommel of his saddle. To her amazement, he put the helmet on his head, gave Micah a look that dared him to say a word, and mounted Rube.

As he passed, Seth grinned at Claire and winked, giving her an overpowering urge to kiss him then and there. He moved Rube alongside Belle, leaving several feet between the horses to give the side-walkers enough room.

Without Seth there to supervise him, Micah slipped away. Minutes later, four or five cowboys lined the arena, and Micah joined them.

"Ride'm, cowboy!" one of the men yelled at Seth.

Seth jerked around in the direction of the catcall, then scowled at Micah, who hung over the fence, laughing.

Claire felt her face heat up. Micah had summoned them solely to embarrass Seth. She wondered if anything she'd been trying to teach had gotten through to the teen.

"Hey, lookee the almighty Seth Morgan. Is that all you can ride now, Morgan?"

Claire recognized the heckler: Chance Shelton, a young wrangler recently hired at the ranch.

"And a helmet, too. Got soft in your old age, did you?"

A couple of the other cowboys hooted. Claire saw the color rise in Seth's face, but he held his temper. Which was almost more than she could say for herself. She was on the verge of confronting the rowdies, but realized that would only embarrass Seth more, so she bit her tongue and continued her instruction.

"Every one of you slackers get back to work. Right now!" Clint called loudly, coming up behind the cowboys. "I've a good mind to dock your pay."

They jumped down and hurried off, but Clint lingered, watching Seth and Natalie. Claire let them ride, no longer worried about a lesson. The little girl was getting more benefit from Seth's company than any exercises Claire might offer.

• • • •

" Why were they laughing, Seth?" Natalie asked, looking at him with concern.

"Because I'm wearing a helmet. Most cowboys don't wear helmets," Seth said. Once it would have bothered him, but lately his image wasn't the most important thing in his life.

"Pretty dumb, aren't they?" Natalie said.

Seth nodded. "Pretty dumb."

At the end of the lesson, Claire led the way to the barn, where Natalie would help care for her horse before going home.

Seth dismounted outside the arena, took the helmet off and headed that way as well, reins in hand. Clint fell in step beside him. "You've got balls to wear that helmet around here."

Seth grinned, leaned toward him and said in a conspiratorial voice, "Well, Claire's the boss, you know."

Her father laughed. "She's got her ways, don't she?"

"That she does."

"Claire told me you got a report from the surgeon."

"Yeah," Seth said. Lately he had tried to keep bull riding and anything related to it off his mind. But like a parasite, the urge to go back to his old way of life ate away at him at times.

"Good news? Bad? Don't care to talk about it?"

"The leg's healing better than expected."

"That's good. What about the future?"

Seth lifted a shoulder noncommittally. When he had asked Doc Tandy about the possibility of riding again, the surgeon had sounded optimistic—which made Seth thoroughly unhappy. Had he been hoping for a bad prognosis so there would be no decision to make?

"I might not be going back to bull riding."

His relationship with Claire was deepening daily, and he didn't want to ruin that. He just wanted this damn camp to be over so they could share more than stolen kisses and whispered endearments—and he could finally see if he had a chance with her.

"Because of Claire?"

Had Clint deduced that or had she told him?

"Not entirely," he said, wary of Clint's curiosity. "I've got some land, and my brother has been after me to start up a bull-breeding operation." That much was true. Lane had the know-how and Seth had the contacts. He figured he could get their bulls into the smaller shows without a problem from the get-go, but it would take a lot of money and time and some good stock to get the business off the ground.

The thought crossed his mind that Claire didn't like anything about ranching, but surely she didn't expect him to give up everything. He had to make a living.

On the other hand, he hadn't actually asked Claire if she'd be willing to live on a ranch with him. There was so much they needed to discuss. That might be a deal breaker, too. What then?

For the first time, he saw the wisdom of his father's admonition to go to college, just in case. Back then, "just in case" had meant nothing to him. How times changed.

"That's fine, son. As long as it's your decision and not somebody else's."

Seth slowed. The decision would be his—wouldn't it?

Clint adjusted his hat and strode off.

After Seth unsaddled Rube, he glanced around for his hat. It was gone from the bench where he'd left it. As he searched the area, he caught Micah's eye and saw the devilment there. Damn kid. Nothing but trouble.

"Where's my hat, Micah?" he asked.

"How would *I* know?"

Seth didn't push the point. Sooner or later he'd get the hat back, but it angered him that Micah had taken it. He'd bought that hat, a genuine Resistol, after his first win. Cost him a small fortune. And it had been on his head ever since, through high times and low. Well, he did take it off to shower and sleep, as well as a few other things, but not often.

He doubted Micah could appreciate that. In fact, after dealing with the kid for the past week, he wondered if Micah Abbott appreciated anything.

CHAPTER FOURTEEN

CLINT SAT ON THE back steps of his house, staring at the shadows falling across the valley, thinking about what was going on between Seth and his daughter. He'd seen no inappropriate behavior from either of them, but the way they looked at each other, and Seth's indecision about returning to bull riding, pretty much told the story.

But how long would that relationship last once Seth's leg was strong again and the urge to ride came back full force? Claire wasn't likely to change her mind about rodeos and ranching after all this time.

Clint had long ago come to terms with his part in his son's death, but Claire still blamed him, something she'd no doubt picked up from her mother. His daughter had been too young to understand that he was trying to shape Cody into a man. A woman could sit around and piddle with crayons, but as far as Clint was concerned, a real man would never be able to take care of a family that way. Maybe he'd been wrong, but the past was past and he couldn't bring Cody back. Neither could Claire, no matter how much she helped other teenagers or avoided rodeos. Cody's death had been a tragic accident, caused by the boy's rashness, not by his involvement in a rodeo. How long would it take Claire to see that?

If she was in love, though, Clint didn't want her hurt. That bull rider would no more be around when she needed him than the wind sighing through the treetops. Once a cowboy was bit by that bug, he never recovered. Clint shook his head. She should have fallen for somebody more her type.

Footsteps approached and Clint half hoped it was Claire coming—they could have a little talk. Instead, Rosie's plump figure appeared around the house. She held a food storage container in her hands.

"Clint, why are you sitting out here in the dark?"

"Just thinking."

"I brought you some leftovers so you wouldn't have to bother cooking."

"I'm getting fat off your leftovers," he said with a grin, patting his stomach, "but I ain't complaining."

Rosie sat down beside him, setting the dish on the top step.

"Nice evening," she said. "Claire's camp seems to be going great guns. They were laughing and cutting up in the dining room when I took over the food."

"Was Seth around?"

"Seth's always around. She hired a good one in him. From the way she talked at first, I was afraid he might not be the best choice."

Clint grunted.

"What? You don't like him?"

"Oh, I like him fine. But I wonder if Claire don't like him too much."

"You noticed that, did you?" Rosie laid a hand on Clint's arm. "Why are you worried? He seems like a nice young man. Polite, responsible."

"Bull rider." Normally Clint held his business close to his vest, but he was truly worried about Claire, and he knew he could trust Rosie. She was as tight-lipped as a sealed Mason jar.

"So? Jon was a bull rider and it doesn't seem to have ruined him for life. His marriage to Kaycee is rock solid."

"Jon did okay, and he quit when he got married the first time. I ain't so sure about Seth. That kid's had the top of the mountain within his reach, and it's hard to give that up. I've talked to him a few times and he's got this fire in him to ride like none I ever seen. And right now he's trying to put it out, and I don't know that he can—or ought to."

Rosie tightened her grip on his arm. "You think Claire pressured him?"

"Either that or he just knows she won't put up with it." Clint had told Rosie about Cody's death and the subsequent divorce after they'd started keeping company, so she knew about Claire's aversion to rodeo.

"They'll work it out, one way or another."

"I hate to see her get hurt."

"I imagine she's broken up with boyfriends before this. Besides, he might not hurt her. Might be the fire for her is hotter than the fire for a bull." Rosie giggled. "My, my, I'm being risqué, aren't I?"

"You keep talking like that and I'll have to shoot the boy."

He looked at Rosie's smooth round face, always flushed from working or baking or just bustling around in general. She was never still, never let the devil find her hands idle. Rosie had become indispensable in the Rider household. And she was smart. A lot sharper with book learning than Clint, and just about as good with numbers. Plus a whole lot better at interacting with and understanding people than he was.

He put his hand on hers and she laid her other hand on top in a comforting gesture. He liked the feel of his rough, callused hand sandwiched between her small, warm ones. Somehow it made things better. More hopeful.

"She'll be all right," Rosie said softly.

"I want her to be happy."

"It's her life. Let her live it, mistakes and all."

"Uh," Clint grunted, his jaw working. "Worries me about the boy, too. He don't want to give up what he loves to do, and how long is he going to be happy trying to live his life to please somebody else? I ain't never done that."

Rosie was quiet beside him. His own words gave him pause.

After a while he said, "And I guess I lost a wife and son 'cause of it."

Rosie patted him on the knee as she rose. "Seth seems like a good man. And Claire's got a rare gift of empathy."

"So I ought to mind my own business, you're saying?"

"Exactly." Rosie gave him a peck on the lips before she turned back toward the house. "By the way, the Riders are taking all the kids to town next weekend for the rodeo. Thought you and I might take a picnic out to the meadow."

Clint grinned, recalling the last picnic Rosie had taken him on. "Sounds like a mighty fine idea to me."

· · · ·

"SETH'S SO ARROGANT," Micah told Annie the next morning as he pushed a wheelbarrow loaded with hay down the barn aisle. With no major infractions during the first week and a half of camp, the adults' strict supervision had slacked off a little, which suited Micah fine. He figured he'd behaved himself so far, and found he liked camp a lot more than he did his own home. But being near Annie all the time tested his willpower.

Today he'd made sure their route took them toward the more iso-lated corner last. The cowboy in charge was busy in another barn, and Annie never paid attention to the route, just followed along with Mic-ah, distributing the feed.

"And he's just a has-been," Micah added. "I heard him tell Clint he might quit bull riding. I hate quitters."

Annie walked beside him with a pail of oats in each hand. "He's a nice guy."

"Yeah, real nice. He's getting it on with our wonderful camp direc-tor, too, you know."

"Claire? You're crazy."

"Don't you see them ride off together every morning? Just like to-day, and they're not back yet. What do you think they're doing all this time?"

"Therapy on Seth's leg. And anyway, if they're in love, I think it's sweet. They're both nice."

"Both do-gooders. And I hate do-gooders."

Annie looked at him. "Why do you hate anybody who tries to help you?"

"You wouldn't understand."

The two teens were progressing down the aisle, leaving hay and oats for the livestock as they went. Micah was finally getting used to the smell of horse and cow manure, grain and hay. At first he'd found the odors repugnant, but now he was beginning to look forward to starting the day in the barns. Maybe it was Annie's company.

More and more he wanted to know what those football players had found under her clothes, what it felt like to hold her and kiss her. The first day at camp she'd turned up her nose at him just like in school, but since then, she'd loosened up a lot. Claire's classes and activities were...*enlightening*—yeah, that was the word, Micah grudgingly admitted, though he never said so aloud.

In fact, he had begun to wish Annie hadn't screwed all those guys, because he felt good talking to her. Not just because she was really pretty, with soft blond hair and bright blue eyes, but because she listened and didn't make fun of him.

When they reached the back end of the barn, where the partially opened door led to an expanse of pastureland, his wheelbarrow was empty. Annie's pails were, too. *Perfect.*

She plunked them into the wheelbarrow. "Guess we'd better get more feed and finish up the last barn."

Micah nonchalantly moved between her and the door, effectively trapping her in an alcove used to store barn implements. "Why don't we just stay in here awhile?"

"No, I don't want to stay," she said, her eyes shifting to the door and back as he moved closer.

"Come on, Annie, let's get to know each other better."

"I know you well enough. Now let me by."

"No, you don't know me at all. Or how good I'll make you feel." Micah braced an arm on either side of her, confining her against the wall. He bent to kiss her and she jerked her head to one side.

"Let me go or I'm gonna scream!"

"Don't do that." Micah made his voice low and persuasive. "Hey, I just want a little of what Brad got, that's all. I heard—"

Smack!

Micah's head jerked back at Annie's hard slap. When she shoved against his chest with all her might, he caught her by the wrists. Sheesh, he hadn't asked for anything she hadn't given freely before. "You know you want it, Annie. You gave it to all those other guys. And I'm as good as they are."

He forced a kiss on her as she struggled in his grip. She tried to scream, but he muffled her attempts with his mouth. Then she started to cry. Tears streamed unchecked down her face. Startled, Micah drew back a few inches.

"Please don't, Micah," she sobbed. "Please. I never did that!"

"What do you mean? Everybody said—"

"Brad lied. They all lied. What you heard were lies."

Lies? No! *She* was lying. Micah hesitated. But what if she wasn't? He knew the influence that jock had over his teammates. What if...what if all this time...

"Did he...like...rape you?"

Annie flushed bright red but shook her head. "No. He got really drunk and tried to, but I fought him off and he passed out."

"Are you telling the truth?"

"Yes. Let me go, Micah, you're hurting me."

He hadn't been aware of how much he'd tightened his grip on her wrists as he'd realized how wrong he'd been about her. But before he could release her, an arm like a band of iron clamped around his throat, and he was dragged backward. Sputtering to draw in a breath, he grabbed at it, trying to claw it loose.

"Go to the dorm, Annie," Seth ordered, as he dragged Micah down the barn aisle.

Unable to dislodge the cords of muscle around his neck, Micah whispered hoarsely, "I...can't...breathe!"

"Why do think you deserve to breathe?" Seth growled in his ear.

"He wasn't hurting me, Seth, I swear!" Annie cried, following them.

"Let me go." Seth loosened his grip and Micah managed to gasp, "You're killing me."

Seth turned him loose inside an empty box stall. "What the hell were you doing?" he demanded.

"I just wanted a kiss," the boy said defensively. "She's okay. I didn't hurt her."

"She didn't look okay," Seth said.

"Annie, tell him!"

"Seth, really, he didn't hurt me." But she was chaffing her wrists where Micah had gripped her.

"So I see," Seth replied. "Go find Claire, Annie."

"No, please, don't tell her," the girl said.

"I don't have any choice. Now go on."

Annie ran from the barn, sobbing.

Seth closed the door of the stall behind them.

"If I ever catch you so much as looking at her crooked again while you're at this camp, I'll take you apart."

Micah forced a short laugh. "You can't take me," he taunted. "Not with that bad leg. You wouldn't have a chance."

"You don't think so?" Seth growled.

Micah felt a tremor of anxiety. Seth looked mad enough to kill right now, even if he did have just one good leg.

Still, Micah sneered. "You're banging the director. Why shouldn't I get a little, too?"

"What the hell are you talking about?" Seth said, crowding closer. His hands were knotted into hard fists at his sides and his face had turned a dark red.

Convinced he'd hit close to home, Micah spoke with bravado. "Just what I said."

Seth backed him into the wall, and Micah knew he'd gone too far. Expecting to feel one of those clenched fists in his face any second, he cringed. But Seth only slammed the boards beside Micah's head, making him jump in fright.

"You listen to me and listen good," Seth snarled, his fist still almost embedded in the wood beside Micah's ear. "If you think I won't hog-tie you, dump you in my truck and throw you out on your mother's doorstep so fast you won't know what hit you, just say something like *that* again—or bother Annie.... Understand? And you've just been docked twenty points and a cowboy hat."

"But I earned that hat!"

"Yeah, well, you stole my hat and now I've got yours. I ought to dock all your points until you bring mine back."

Fury raced through Micah's body. This SOB couldn't do that to him. Twenty points! He had only forty left after spending the points for the fine white cowboy hat, and those were going toward the tooled cowboy boots waiting for him. If Seth took half of them, he'd never earn those boots! Everybody else already had theirs, but because of the damned horse fiasco, he hadn't been awarded all his points. He opened his mouth to protest more.

"And if you say another word, I promise you I'll take away every point you've got. Now get to work. I want every stall in our horse barn mucked out before noon. And as soon as I talk to Claire, you're going to apologize to Annie."

Micah thought he might explode but didn't dare chance losing everything. And he did want to apologize to Annie. Seeing her cry had made a profound impression on him. He clamped his mouth shut. Seth nodded for him to get out of there and Micah took the opportunity to flee.

But not without his thoughts racing about how he was going to win Annie's trust—and get even with Seth. And he was sure as hell wasn't going to give him back his hat now!

CHAPTER FIFTEEN

"CLAIRE?"

She turned from the paperwork on her desk to find Annie in the office doorway. The girl's trembling voice and red eyes frightened Claire.

"What's wrong? Annie, are you okay?"

Tears streamed down the girl's face. "Seth made me come," she sobbed.

Claire crossed the room to lead her to a chair. "Tell me what happened. Are you hurt?"

Annie used her shirttail to wipe her eyes. "It wasn't as bad as it looked, I swear," she said, her voice so low it was barely audible.

"What?" Claire's anxiety level was approaching redline. The girl wasn't injured in any obvious way, so she forced herself to wait for Annie to talk.

"Micah tried to kiss me in the barn and I...I wouldn't let him."

"Did he hurt you?" she asked.

"Not really, just squeezed my wrists really hard."

Claire reached for her arm and Annie pulled away at first, then relented and allowed her to raise her sleeve. Slight bruises stood out on Annie's pale skin where Micah had grabbed her. "So you fought him off?"

"Yes, and he said I was easy, and I told him I wasn't and that Brad and the others lied."

"Okay. Did he turn you loose?"

"He was going to, but Seth grabbed him from behind and pulled him away. He wasn't hurting me anymore. He believed me."

"I'm so sorry this happened, Annie. Micah will be disciplined. He won't bother you again, I promise."

"I don't want him to be punished. I don't know what Seth was going to do to him in the barn, but he was yelling at Micah and he shut the stall door with them inside."

"You wait right here. Don't leave the room. I'm going to see about Micah."

"Oh, thank you!"

Claire hurried out, anxious that Seth had taken the discipline into his own hands. It turned out one wasn't far from the other. Micah was mucking out stalls in the horse barn and hauling manure to the big heap outside. Seth was sitting on a nearby fence, keeping watch. Micah looked pale and scared, but unharmed. Claire had no sympathy for him at the moment.

As he turned from dumping another load of soil on the pile, he caught Claire's gaze. He looked away quickly and hustled back into the barn with his barrow.

"I guess Annie found you?" Seth said grimly as Claire reached him. "How is she?"

"She's okay now. She says Micah wasn't hurting her."

"Could've fooled me. He had a death grip on her wrists. Had her pinned against the wall, trying to kiss her."

"She told me that, but said by the time you got there, they were talking."

"Huh. I probably screwed up, anyway," Seth said, his gaze fixed on the open barn door.

"How so?"

"I was so mad, I literally dragged him off her."

"I don't have a problem with that," Claire said, "under the circumstances."

"In a choke hold?" Seth glanced down at her from his perch on the fence.

She rubbed her forehead wearily. "Hmm, not so good, maybe. But I saw the bruises on Annie's arm, so I think your action is defensible." She was keyed up inside, worried not only about Micah, but about Seth's physical reaction—which was just what her father would have done. Still, her main concern was for the two teenagers.

"Annie doesn't want Micah punished."

"He needs to be. I'd send his butt home, myself," Seth said. "But I know that's not what you want to do."

"I want to help him, not ostracize him. Besides it's going to be hard to send him home right now. Remember I told you about Terri Harper, the woman who was going to try to help his mother? Well, Mrs. Abbott has agreed to go into rehab tomorrow. And their trailer is being condemned, so that Terri can arrange for a small rental in town. So he'd fall under Child Protection Services, and he's got more on his plate than he can handle as it is."

"I didn't know all that was going on," Seth said. "I guess we've got to keep him, then. But I did dock him twenty points and take away his hat. Will you back me up on that?"

"I will, but I have to ask. Did you take away his hat to retaliate because you think he took yours?"

"Maybe a little," Seth admitted.

"You know that's half the points he had left after paying for the hat."

"I know. I threatened to take them all away when he talked back to me. If he straightens up, I'll give him ways to earn them back. But only if he changes his attitude."

"Okay, I'm with you."

Micah emerged from the barn again, wheelbarrow loaded. He set it down for a moment, wiped his brow and looked at Claire, as if she might give him a reprieve.

Instead, Seth spoke up. "Get a drink of water from the cooler in the tack room and get back to work. You've got a five-minute water break. And I estimate about five more stalls to clean afterward."

"Come *on*, cleaning stalls is not my assignment."

"It is now. And you're wasting your water break. You've got four minutes now."

"Claire?" Micah whined.

"Clock's ticking," Seth said.

Micah glared at both of them, but when Claire didn't intervene, he stomped off to the tack room.

"I've got the perfect punishment for him," Seth said when Micah was gone.

"What's that?" Claire asked with interest, willing to try just about anything to keep Micah at camp.

"Until further notice, he's going to be my shadow. With me every day, every free hour. The only break he gets is when he's in the dorm room. And I've reassigned his chores to cleaning stalls, beginning now."

Claire smiled wryly. "And I guess there's no need for Jon's men to clean out our barn, since Micah seems to enjoy it so much."

"My thought exactly. And I'm not averse to a little fence sitting now and then. Besides, it wasn't that long ago I was a lot like him."

"Were you really? In trouble all the time?"

"Not anything real bad. My dad and brothers would have booted me to kingdom come if I'd gotten in trouble with the law. But I had my share of visits to the principal's office."

"Then maybe you're just what he needs."

"Tell *him* that," Seth said. "Oh, and by the way, he thinks you and I are getting it on."

"What?" Claire's voice rose two octaves. "That's just great. Where did that come from?"

"Search me. But I'm sure he's going to hit us with both barrels when he gets the chance."

"I'll bring the flak jackets," Claire said, not looking forward to tonight, when she planned to talk to Micah.

• • • •

"MICAH'S FINE," Claire told Annie when she returned to her office. "Seth's got him mucking out stalls. He just didn't want Micah to hurt you."

"I know. But I want you and Seth to know that Micah was listening to me. He believed me." Annie's eyes were shining with a glow that hadn't been there before. "Nobody at school would believe me about what happened, but Micah...well, he's changed since he's been here."

That surprised Claire. She hadn't noticed any change and had begun to think the youth might be a lost cause, after all.

"What did happen at school, Annie?" Claire asked. "All I get is general behavioral information, like grades falling, acting out in class, if there have been scrapes with outside authorities, but not the details. So all I know is you began to have problems in school after an incident last fall. It would help if you told me what the incident was."

Annie stared at the rough wooden floor. Her hands trembled in her lap and tears ran down her cheeks again. She sniffled. Claire went to the bathroom and brought back a box of tissue for her.

When she calmed a little, Annie said, "The captain of the football team told everybody that...he said that...he...we, you know...*did it*...over and over. And that the other football players did, too." Her voice broke, but she managed to go on. "He said I wanted more...that I was a nympho." She began sobbing again. "And everybody believed him. And now they all think I'm a whore."

Claire took the teen's hands in hers. "Did he rape you, Annie? Or give you something like a date-rape drug so that you don't remember?"

Annie shook her head. "No, I remember everything. But he might as well have. Nobody believes me, except Mary Lou. Since then she's become my best friend. She was acting out at school to defend me and so she could come with me to camp."

That was a darn good best friend, Claire thought. No wonder they'd had none of the trouble they expected from Mary Lou. She'd had her reasons for bad behavior all along.

"So you never had sex with him? Exactly what *did* happen?"

Annie blushed and shook her head. "No, I never did—with him or anybody else. I really fell for him at the first of the school year and he said he liked me, too. He asked me out and after a few dates, he wanted to go steady. I was so excited to be dating the most popular boy in school. But one night after a big game, we went to a party at another player's house. The parents weren't around, and there was a lot of booze and drugs. Brad got drunk and we went to a bedroom to make out. But he wanted more and tried to make me do what he wanted. I fought him off and he passed out on the bed. I left the party and called my mom to pick me up. I didn't tell her what happened—and don't you tell her, either, please, because it would just tear her up to know all this."

"I'm not going to tell her, but I think you should. You need her support and her help to get things straightened out at school. Besides, she knows something is wrong because of your grades. I'm sure she's already worried about you. It might ease her mind to know how well you've handled the situation."

"I guess," Annie said. "But I don't want my mom hurt."

"We'll talk about that more before you go home, okay? So this guy told a lie at school about what happened, and his buddies backed him up?"

"Yes, they all acted like jerks and went along with him. And since they're such big heroes around school, nobody would take my side. I never had a lot of friends, anyway...."

"Did you tell Miss Haynes or your principal?"

"No, because everybody would just hate me worse for getting Brad in trouble. Besides nobody would believe me, so what's the point."

Claire lifted the girl's chin gently. "I believe you, Annie."

"Are you sure you're not just saying that? Because you don't have to, really. I've learned pretty much to ignore what people think about me. But Micah...I don't want Micah to believe that stuff." Annie was quiet for a minute, then looked at Claire through swollen eyes. "I really don't want you to throw him out of camp or anything. He just did that because of what he heard."

"Micah was wrong. No matter what he's heard, he had no right to force you to do anything."

"He stopped when I told him to. Honestly, he did."

"Micah needs to learn to respect boundaries. Seth has reassigned his chores."

"Okay, if that's all you do to him."

"Now dry those tears before you go out."

Annie's lips twitched into a slight smile and she dabbed at her eyes with a tissue.

"And, Annie," Claire said, as the girl rose to go, "anytime you need to talk, I'm here to listen."

Annie caught her around the neck and hugged her hard. "Thank you so much for believing me, Claire!"

· · · ·

AFTER DINNER, when the campers normally gathered around the table to chat and play board games, Claire took Micah to her office to get his side of the story. Then she would summon Annie and Seth.

Micah slouched in the folding chair opposite her desk, legs spread, arm slung over the back of the chair—I'm a tough guy in trouble again. His anger seemed to fill the room.

"Do you want to tell me what happened today between you and Annie?" Claire asked.

He didn't answer at first. Then he snorted and said, "She wanted to make out."

"Micah, you and I both know that's not true. Annie had bruises on her arm."

"Maybe she got them working in the barn," he hedged.

"Micah."

He narrowed his eyes at her. "Prove I did it."

"I'm sure you realize that I talked to Annie, and Seth saw you."

"Yeah, Seth just about choked me to death. And he mighta thought he saw something, but he didn't. I didn't do a thing to Annie."

"Let's stop beating around the bush and talk about why you tried to force her to do something she didn't want to do. And what we're going to do about it."

Micah picked at a flaking chip of paint on the edge of the metal chair. "Why don't you just leave me alone? I don't want your help or anybody else's."

"I think you're worth the effort," Claire said honestly.

Micah's eyes were riveted on the seat as he worked at scratching off the paint. "Your time's better spent on somebody else—like Annie."

"I'm trying to help her, too, but I think you could have set her back a lot today."

He looked up in surprise. "What do you mean?"

"I mean she was starting to feel good about herself again and you put her right back in the situation she was in at school."

"Did she tell you that?" he said. His familiar hostile mask was back.

"No. I'm putting myself in her shoes."

Micah snorted again. "Okay. I kissed her and she started crying and that's all. I didn't hurt her or force her to do anything else. And I wasn't gonna."

"Well, what you *are* going to do is apologize to Annie, and then we're going to discuss your punishment."

Micah slid lower in his chair, arms folded belligerently across his chest.

Claire left her office to collect Seth and Annie. She returned with them moments later.

"Sit there, Annie." Claire motioned to a chair a few feet from Micah's.

Annie sat, her chest rising and falling rapidly. She wouldn't look at anyone.

"Micah has something to say to you, Annie." Claire turned to him and nodded.

The boy refused to talk at first, then muttered almost under his breath, "I'm sorry about this morning, Annie."

The girl darted a look at him, then ducked her head again.

"Annie," Claire said, "here's the way it is. You can accept Micah's apology and we'll get past today and move on. Or you can say the word and I'll have Seth take Micah home tomorrow."

"Let him stay," she whispered.

"Thank you, Annie." Claire smiled at her. "I appreciate your courage. You can go now."

Annie left the room quickly.

"So, I've done what you wanted, Madame Camp Director," Micah said with cutting sarcasm. "May I go, too?"

Claire saw Seth stiffen and the color rise into his face.

"No," she said, "you may not. We went over the rules the first day of camp and I was very clear about disrespecting other campers. If you break the rules, you suffer the consequences. That's life."

"Life sucks."

"Life's what you make of it, Micah," Seth said, "and you just made yours a lot harder."

The boy scowled as Claire explained the new restrictions on him.

"That's crap!" he shouted when she told him Seth would be his constant companion. "I hate Seth and he hates me. You can't stick me with him 24/7. Besides, he tried to kill me."

"You will speak civilly to me and to Seth," Claire said, knowing she was walking a thin line between helping Micah and losing him. "Seth told me how he restrained you. I heard both his and Annie's version of what happened, and I think under the circumstances, he did what he felt he had to do. I wish it hadn't happened that way. But then, I wish you hadn't tried to impose yourself on Annie."

"He took half my points away, and my hat, too," Micah whined. "And you expect me to clean all those stables all by myself?"

"Yes," Claire said. "That's exactly what we expect."

"No way."

"Okay, then, I'll have Seth drive you home tomorrow morning. Be ready at five-thirty. I'd like to get your dismissal paperwork done and have you gone before we start the day."

Micah paled and even Seth looked at her in confusion. She was playing her trump card, and if it didn't work, she was going to have to explain to him about his mother and social services. She felt, at the moment, that she might have done the boy more harm than good, however unintended.

The teenager swallowed hard, his eyes darting from her to Seth and back. Knuckles white, he gripped the edge of the seat, where he'd managed to clear the paint off an inch-long stretch of metal during the time he'd been sitting there. He shoved a hand through his long hair and heaved a sigh of surrender that sounded almost like a sob.

"Okay, whatever," he said. "I'll do the extra work. I don't want to go home."

"And you'll work with Seth."

"Whatever. Just tell him he can't choke me to death out behind the barn and call it an accident."

The tension in the room deflated. Micah slumped in the chair, giving up all pretense of a fight.

"I'll be sure he understands that," Claire said, suppressing a tiny smile.

"Let's go, then," Seth said.

"I feel like I've just pulled ten in the pen," Micah muttered as he preceded Seth out the door.

"That's exactly what we're trying to avoid, Micah," Seth said as they walked the short distance to the dorm. "Thank your lucky stars."

• • • •

THE NEXT MORNING at breakfast, Seth entered the dining hall to find Micah sitting at a distance from the others. Seth certainly understood Annie's reluctance to be close to him, but had all the others decided to snub him, too? Even Claire?

She rolled her eyes at Seth when he came in and jerked her head slightly toward Micah. So something else was afoot. Seth filled his plate with scrambled eggs, biscuits and sausage from Rosie's excellent breakfast buffet, then poured himself coffee and orange juice. Instead of sitting near Claire as he usually did, he took a seat in the ample space surrounding Micah. And immediately turned his face away and squeezed his eyes closed until the reek became bearable. Micah was wearing the same clothes he'd worn yesterday when he'd cleaned the stalls. A night lying in a crumpled heap on the floor had not sweetened them in the least, and it appeared Micah had not showered or shaved this morning, either.

Seth fought the urge to move away like the others had, but he knew Micah was playing games, trying to be as obnoxious as he could. Seth fell to eating and attempted to avoid gagging with each bite. The others watched the pair with curious expressions.

"What's the matter?" Micah taunted when the silence in the room grew palpable. "Don't like the way I smell?"

Seth cocked an eyebrow at him. "Micah, I grew up around livestock all my life. You don't smell any worse than some bulls I've known." Seth put another forkful of eggs in his mouth as the room erupted in laughter.

Micah turned red to the tips of his ears. "Those bulls you're not going to be riding anymore?" he taunted. "Cripple."

The room fell silent once more. Pressure built to an explosive level in Seth's chest, suffusing his body with heat. But he wasn't going to let this punk kid get to him. He pointed his fork toward Micah's food.

"Better be eating. Lots of work for you today."

When they finished, they scraped their plates into a slop bucket and left them in the large dishpan for Rosie and her helpers—the young Rider girls—to clear away. As they left the building, Seth stepped into his room, grabbed Micah's confiscated hat from the dresser where he'd put it last night, and set it on his own head. Seth's leg barely bothered him in the mornings anymore, though it worsened by night fall. He caught up to Micah, who seemed determined to leave him in the dust.

The teen cast a quick sidelong look at him, then stopped short, staring. "You're wearing my hat!"

"Looks better on me than it does on you," Seth said, readjusting it at a jaunty angle.

"You are a lousy, crazy son of—"

Seth cut him a look.

"Cowboy," Micah finished. "That's not fair."

"Let's make a deal. You return my hat, in the same shape as when it got 'lost,' and I'll give yours back ahead of time."

"You can't even prove I've got your hat. There were lots of people around the barn that day."

"However you want it, Micah. I like this hat fine. Get busy."

Micah set to work in the stables. Seth had been lying when he told Claire he liked fence-sitting. In fact, he hated to be idle, but he wasn't about to ease Micah's punishment the first day, so he found work in the tack room, polishing the already clean saddles and bridles to a sheen. The horses were grazing in the pasture, eliminating the time spent transferring each one to a holding pen while the stall was cleaned. Micah worked diligently and was soon done, smelling no worse after the work than he had before he started.

"Good job," Seth said when he'd inspected the stalls. "I've got something else for you to do now."

"You planning to work me to death, instead of choking me?"

Seth laughed. "You look like you can take it. Gets you in better shape to fight me if you ever have to."

"I'd take you down now if it'd get me out of this grunt work."

"Nope. You'd be at a disadvantage. Better bulk up a little more."

Micah muttered something under his breath but didn't challenge him again. Seth took off the boy's hat, swiped his brow with a shirt-sleeve and reset the hat in place, his movements slow and deliberate just to aggravate Micah.

Then he led him to the large pre-fab metal building that served as a workshop and repair shop for the ranch equipment. He introduced Micah to Sonny, the cowboy who worked as the ranch mechanic.

"Your second chore every day," Seth told Micah, "is to sweep the floors here early morning and late afternoon and do whatever clean up Sonny needs. I'll be back for you."

When Seth returned for him, the boy looked whipped.

"I think I'll shower before lunch," he muttered.

"Nope," Seth said. "You wanted to dress that way today, so you can just keep 'em on until tonight."

"That's not fair!" Micah retorted.

"Fair or not, it's the way things are. You get a new chance every morning to determine what you're going to do with your day and your life. This was your decision today and you live with it."

During lunch Micah spewed his troubles to anyone who would listen and blamed Seth for not letting him clean up before lunch. As they were leaving the dining room, Claire called Seth aside.

"Aren't you being a little rough on him?" she asked. "And the rest of us, too, considering how he smells."

"No, I'm not. He needs to learn to live with his decisions, good or stupid."

"Still…"

"Claire, you have got to stop coddling that kid if you want to keep him out of prison. He's sharp enough to take advantage of weakness."

"Are you saying I'm weak?" she demanded, frowning deeply. "Just because I want him treated decently?"

"You'd like to *love* him out of his problems, and that's fine sometimes," Seth replied. "But right now he needs to work them out himself. You wanted me to be a role model for him, so let me. You've got to trust me—he'll be okay."

Claire didn't seem appeased.

"I'm trying to do things your way," Seth said, "but in this case I think Micah needs a stronger arm."

"You better be right. You just better be right."

CHAPTER SIXTEEN

EACH NIGHT AFTER DINNER, everybody hung around in the dining room, enjoying games and music and conversation. Since the incident on Wednesday, Micah had been forced to sit aside with Seth, but on Sunday, to start the week on a positive note, Seth turned him loose. Micah edged over to the group of kids, including Annie, who sat around one of the dining tables playing Yahtzee. Seth watched him closely but didn't interfere. Sooner or later Micah was going to have to find his way back into the good graces of the others.

"Is it okay if I sit down?" he asked, his hands jammed into his back pockets.

"Sure," Jason said immediately. The boy looked hopeful and at the same time a little wary. No doubt he'd like to have the older, bigger teen for a friend, but was still afraid of rejection.

Micah hesitated, shuffling from one foot to another. "Is it okay with you, Annie?"

She dipped her head over the playing cup in her hand. "I guess so," she mumbled, then threw the dice—too hard, it turned out. One shot off the table, hitting Micah.

Jason and Mary Lou laughed at the expression on his face. Annie turned beet-red. Micah scowled for a moment, then plucked the fallen die from the floor and plopped it back in the cup in Annie's hand.

"You get to throw again," he said with a grin, sitting down with them.

Annie sent him a shy smile and gathered the dice.

The game resumed. Sitting beside Seth on the other side of the room, Claire caught his hand under the table and leaned against him for a moment. She smiled and Seth's heart quickened. Nobody's smile had ever done that to him.

He had been trying for days to sort out the emotions rampaging inside him. He wanted Claire more than he'd ever wanted any woman before. There was nothing rational about it. He simply craved her all the time and having to keep his distance because of camp was wearing on him.

Did he love her?

He didn't have a lot of experience with anything but lust when it came to women. With him, it had always been a sexual thing where he took what they were willing to give. But Claire had changed everything, turned his world on end. He didn't press her for sex, even though he was dying to touch her again, to taste her sweet lips, to please her in every way. He'd never felt so protective of a woman, so attuned to the slightest nuance of expression of the lilt of her voice when she spoke his name. So aware of her presence in his world—and so possessive that he didn't appreciate the slightest glance from the other cowboys.

On top of that, he was on the brink of giving up the one thing in his life he knew and loved. Just for her. And somehow, the sacrifice seemed okay.

While the teenagers were occupied with their game, Seth tugged Claire's hand and they slipped quietly out the door. He led her to the end of the long porch, where the overhead lights didn't reach.

"Just wanted a minute alone with you," he said, drawing her into his arms. The moonlight reflected in her eyes, turning them to pools of liquid. "I'll be glad to have you to myself when camp's over."

He tangled his hand in her hair and pulled her face close to his. His tongue teased her lips until she opened for him.

"Seth, we shouldn't," she protested weakly.

"We can hear them if they get restless," he said, then brought her mouth back to his. This time he wouldn't allow their lips to part long enough for her to answer.

Happy to have her in his arms in the darkness, Seth had to content himself with just kissing her, but he wanted so much more. He needed her to fill the strange emptiness inside that nagged him lately. Maybe Micah's misbehavior and the sense that nothing they did was helping the boy left Seth restless, dissatisfied and craving Claire every night—or maybe it was something more personal.

• • • •

T HE NEXT AFTERNOON the campers worked with their horses in the round pen again where they had to put them through their paces: walk, trot, canter, trot, walk. Stop, reverse, and repeat in the other direction. All had made impressive progress except for Micah, who had only spotty success getting Monkey Business past the trotting phase. When he finally got Monkey trotting and called for a canter, the gelding stopped, craned his head toward Micah and blew noisily through his nostrils.

"Trot, damn it." Micah flicked the whip. Monkey snorted again but didn't move.

"Trot!" he repeated, flipping the tip of the whip hard. It struck Monkey's flank. The horse squealed and bolted.

Claire and Seth were off the fence at the same time. She rushed between Micah and the frightened horse. Seth grabbed the boy and hauled him outside the pen.

"I didn't mean to hit him, I swear," Micah said, holding up his hands as if Seth had threatened him.

Claire had made the rules clear. The horses were never to be touched with the whip.

Micah's shoulders slumped. "I shouldn't be here," he said. "I'm messing things up for everybody."

Seth had never seen him so shaken. Angry and rebellious, yes, but not unnerved. The kid seemed close to the breaking point.

"Get busy with your chores. I'll talk to Claire."

"At least you've got an in with her."

"Look, Micah," Seth said testily, "do you want me to help you or not? You're not going to trash-talk and keep me on your side."

"You're on *my* side?" Micah said with a snort.

"I'm trying my best," Seth stated, "but you don't make it easy."

"Can I skip dinner? I'm not hungry."

"No, you come to dinner after you've finished in the garage."

Stifling a response, Micah took off across the stable yard before Claire emerged from the pen, leading Monkey.

"Where's he going?" she asked.

"To do his chores. You know he didn't mean to actually hit the horse."

"He can't let his temper get the best of him when dealing with the horses."

"He's changing, Claire. He's worried about the impact he's having on the others. I know you've got to dock him some points, but as few as you can, okay?"

Claire heaved a long sigh. "I hope you're right. But I'm afraid he's getting worse rather than better."

• • • •

MICAH MISSED HIS JOB of feeding the animals with Annie. After mucking out horse stalls, he always went to help Sonny clean up the repair garage. Usually Seth came along and the two cowboys talked while Micah worked. But today, after hurting Monkey, Micah felt like an outcast. Seth had sent him ahead and hadn't shown up yet, and Sonny wasn't around. Their absence left Micah with a lot of time to think, and his thoughts didn't make him happy. Like always, he'd blown everything. For some reason that mattered to him now. He turned to his work to salve some of the guilt. Sonny always praised him when he did well, so he tried his best.

First he carefully placed the tools on the workbench into their holders on the Peg-Board wall. Then he swept the floor and spot-treated a couple of small spills with ground-up corncob. Tomorrow morning he would sweep that up, too, and put it back in the bin to be reused, before he started mucking out stalls.

For a moment he thought he imagined hearing his name, but it came again in a louder whisper. He turned to find Annie in the doorway, an empty pail in her hand.

"Are you all right?" she asked softly.

Micah shrugged.

"It could have happened to any of us," she told him.

"Not really," Micah said, moving closer. He didn't want to get in more trouble, but he couldn't resist those big blue eyes. "All of you learned to make your horses obey. That Monkey doesn't like me and I'll never make any progress. I think I'm going to hitch a ride home."

"No!" Annie grabbed his arm. "You can't. They won't let you back in school!"

"I don't care. I'll get points docked for hitting the horse. Maybe all of them. And Seth already took my hat away."

"So what? It's just clothes. And you've got time to earn back the points before the end of camp. We're all in this together and you're not going to cop out on us."

"Annie, I'm so sorry for what I did in the barn. I...I really am. I won't ever do that again. And I won't let the others say any more of that crap about you, either."

"Brad just wanted everybody to think he was a big shot. But he passed out drunk."

"You're kidding! Tough Brad passed out?"

"He sure did, and he didn't have all that much to drink. He can't hold his liquor."

Micah chuckled. "Imagine that. The guy gives me grief all the time. It won't happen anymore. And look, if anybody bothers you again, let me know. I'll shut them up."

Annie smiled briefly. "I wouldn't want you to do that. I'd rather you stayed out of trouble. I think you'd be a great guy if you weren't always trying to be bad."

"Look, do me a favor, okay? I hid Seth's hat in the hayloft of the barn. Get it down for me and put it at his place at the table. Then maybe he'll give me back *my* hat."

"Okay, I'll find it." She looked around furtively, then stretched up and gave him a quick peck on the cheek. "Please stay, Micah."

When Annie ran off, Micah couldn't move. His hand went to his cheek, where he imagined he still felt her lips. Could he tough out the rest of the camp, even for Annie? Maybe he'd give it another day, just for her, but if he screwed up again, he had no doubt Seth would kick him out.

That night at dinner, Seth's hat was on the table at his usual seat. Without looking at Micah, he picked the hat up and put it on. He walked into his room and came back with Micah's white hat, plopped it on the kid's head and sat down to eat.

Annie grinned and gave Micah a thumbs-up, and all of a sudden things seemed more right than they had in years.

Micah slept soundly and awoke early. He dressed and slipped out of the dorm room in spite of Seth's nasty duct-tape warning. He was outside and easing the door closed when he realized there wasn't any duct tape on the door at all. That damn Seth. He had Micah's number, all right. How many nights could he have slipped out with nobody knowing?

"Going somewhere?" Seth said from behind him.

Micah jumped and whirled around. Seth had come from the dining room with a bottle of cold water in his hand. He was barefoot, unshaved, wearing sweatpants and a long-sleeve, black shirt with a Pro Bull Riders logo on it. Was he hanging around outside to catch Micah or was it just dumb luck?

"I was going to work early at the garage," Micah said.

"What about breakfast?"

"I was going to come back to eat after I was done in the garage, then try to finish the stables early."

"Why?"

He worried that Seth wouldn't believe him. He felt like that kid who cried wolf all the time.

"Because I want to earn extra points," Micah said truthfully. "I was going to help the others when I was done."

"Good idea," Seth said with a nod. "Get going."

Surprised, Micah didn't wait for him to change his mind. He trotted toward the garage, eager for once to start the day.

Micah picked up the greasy absorbent material from the floor of the garage. He was glad Seth had assigned him here, especially the afternoon when they'd helped Sonny replace a carburetor. Micah soaked up every detail of engine repair he could. Maybe he'd learn enough to fix his dad's rusty old truck.

After breakfast, he rushed to the stables to begin cleaning. Claire hadn't mentioned taking away any more of his points last night, and he hoped he might save himself by working extra hard, if Seth would intervene for him.

To his surprise, Seth was hauling a load of soiled hay to the manure pile.

"What are you doing?" Micah asked. If Seth did his work for him, he wouldn't have a chance to earn his points.

"Helping you finish early."

Micah didn't argue, but he felt disheartened. Inside, he found half the stalls already clean and spread with fresh straw. He grabbed a fork and began on the next enclosure. Between them they finished the barn in less than half the usual time.

"I guess you get half my points today," Micah said.

"Nope. Not a one. You get them all."

Confused, Micah asked, "You kidding?"

"No, not kidding. We're going to take the extra time to make friends with Monkey. Put the tools away and let's go."

Micah's heart sank further. He'd planned to help Annie and Mary Lou with their chores, but he was going to be stuck with a stupid horse—and Seth.

"That horse won't ever get friendly with me."

Seth stopped and turned to him. "He will if you make the effort. But hey, it's your decision. I'm willing to give you some pointers, but if you'd rather not, you can take your chances with him in the round pen."

"Okay. Fine." Micah practically spat out the words. "Let's go."

A few minutes later, he and Seth stood inside the pasture where the camp horses grazed peacefully. Seth gave a short whistle, but it wasn't necessary. His big horse Rube had started toward him the minute he entered the pasture. Seth opened the gate and sent Rube through it to the valley beyond.

"Open the gate when Monkey comes."

"Monkey won't come."

"I'm going to encourage him," Seth said. He moved among the herd until he'd cut Monkey out. The horse obviously wanted to stay with the other horses, but Seth wouldn't let him.

"Open the gate," he repeated.

Monkey bolted through, snorted and ran off.

"What are you doing?" Micah cried. "Claire will kill me for letting Monkey out!"

"He's not going anywhere."

"He'll run away."

"What's the incentive for him to run away? He's a herd animal and his herd is back here. And if he can't get to them, then he'll herd with Rube for the time being—and Rube's not going anywhere without me."

Seth led Micah into the meadow.

"That's just crazy," Micah said.

But sure enough, Monkey had circled to the fence a few hundred yards away and was looking longingly at the herd in the other pasture. Rube grazed close by and his ears flicked constantly toward Seth. Seth sat on the ground, stretching his legs in front of him.

"Sit down," he told Micah.

Micah dropped cross-legged beside him. Still grazing, Rube worked his way slowly away from them. Soon Monkey moved in step, grazing, but looking nervously toward the two humans every few minutes.

"You and Monkey are a lot alike, Micah," Seth said.

"You said that before, but we're not!"

"Yeah, you are. Monkey's an intelligent horse. He's figured out how to outsmart you, just like you think you've learned how to outsmart the adults in your life. But it comes with a price. He gets hit by a whip in anger, and you get punished by the adults. Monkey doesn't run away, because all the security he knows is right here with his herd. You don't run away because, whether it's an ideal situation or not, your mother and your home are the only security you have. Monkey couldn't make it on his own in the wild. And you can't make it on your own in the world."

When Micah started to argue, Seth cut him off. "Trust me, right now you couldn't, not and stay off the streets. Could you?"

Micah's anger deflated as Seth's words sank in. He watched Monkey graze, keeping close to Rube for security. Just like this horse was trapped by his own needs, Micah was trapped in his life. Suddenly he felt defeated, and a little afraid.

"What do I do, Seth? I've screwed up with everybody. Why would they give me another chance?"

"Are you willing to give Monkey another chance?"

"I guess so."

"Bingo," Seth said.

"You think all those people I've pissed off will just welcome me back with open arms?"

"No, I think you're going to have to prove yourself. But I also believe you can do it if you try." Seth watched the horses grazing placidly. "You're old enough to take responsibility for your decisions. That's one thing Claire has going at this camp. She's holding everybody responsible for their own actions."

"Yeah, Claire's pretty cool. Miss Haynes said the only way I could come back to school was by finishing this camp. I almost took off last night."

"Good thing you didn't."

"She said I have to get my grades up and apply to community college."

"Do it."

"I don't know if I want to go to college. I'd rather just get a job."

To Micah's surprise, Seth grew quiet.

Now the grazing horses were moving closer.

"Where'd you go to college?" Micah asked after awhile.

"I didn't," Seth said shortly.

"So why should I?"

Seth leaned forward, his hands massaging his bad leg. He didn't answer immediately. Finally, Seth said, "Because I should have. Now, if I can't ride bulls, I don't have much to fall back on. My father wanted me to go to college and I wouldn't. I passed up that opportunity and there are days now when I really wish I hadn't. I was too young and too stupid to take good advice."

"Well, my old man's not going to be much help from prison."

"So, get help elsewhere. Miss Haynes can help you find money for college. And you've definitely got an advocate in Claire. She really fought to get you into this camp. Don't let her down." Seth looked at him hard. "I saw you talking to Annie yesterday at the garage."

"So?" Micah felt alarmed, expecting worse punishment, or maybe banishment from camp. "I didn't do anything to her. She went there on her own."

"I know, I was watching."

A spy is what he should have been, Micah thought.

"Seems like she forgave you."

"Yeah. Look, I wasn't going to do anything but kiss her that other time. You overreacted."

"You had a vicious grip on that girl. Do I look that dumb?"

"Okay, I admit, at first I really thought she'd give in easy. I thought...from all I'd heard...Then she started crying and I was honestly about to turn her loose when you tried to choke me to death."

"Well, if you've got any more ideas about taking advantage of her, back off now."

"I swear I don't," Micah said quickly. "I...I really kind of like her."

By now Rube and Monkey were grazing only a few yards away.

"Should I go get him?" Micah asked.

"Nope. You wouldn't catch him. Just sit here and don't look at him. He'll get curious after a while."

"We're missing lunch."

"That's true and I'm hungry." Seth pushed up from the ground. Micah started to do the same, but Seth laid a hand on his shoulder. "You're staying here."

"I'm hungry, too."

"Yes, but my horse likes me."

As if to prove that, Seth whistled softly and Rube lifted his head and moved toward them. Monkey followed a short distance, then stopped.

"That's not fair! You've had that horse a long time."

"You've got to start somewhere. You need to stay here until you and Monkey come to a higher level of understanding."

"That could take forever," Micah protested.

"Could. I'll bring you something to eat."

"You're leaving me all alone out here with *him?*"

"Yep."

"Suppose I run away. Or Monkey does. Suppose we're just not here when you get back?"

"Micah, the only one you really hurt by bad decisions is yourself. Why don't you make friends with the horse while you've got the opportunity? There won't be anybody to criticize or instruct. You're on your own to make something work. Here."

Seth handed Micah the halter and lead rope he'd brought.

"This is what you do. Don't go after Monkey. Wait until he comes to you on his own, talk to him and let him graze away if he wants to. Don't try to catch him."

"Why?"

"Because you want him to trust you. He doesn't right now, because you confused him in the pen. A horse like Monkey always looks for a leader and I'm taking Rube away, so sooner or later Monkey's going to have to rely on you to let him go back to his buddies."

"Fine," Micah said, resigned to his fate, but not happy. "Then what?"

"He's been trained. He knows how to behave. He's just giving you a hard time because he doesn't consider you a leader. When he's finally willing to put his head into the halter, just fasten it quietly, talk to him and walk to the gate. But don't open it until he's calm and you know you're in control."

"What if he doesn't come?"

"Then you've got a long road ahead of you." Seth must have sensed Micah's rising fury. "And if you're angry, even at me, you'll lose the battle."

Micah clenched his teeth, breathing hard and fast through his nose, but he didn't retort for fear of worse punishment than sitting in a field with a stupid horse. Now he wished he'd kept Seth's hat. In fact, he wished he'd buried it in the middle of the manure pile.

CHAPTER SEVENTEEN

A COUPLE OF DAYS LATER, everybody cheered as Micah led Monkey through the gate into the round pen and put him through his paces. Not a flawless performance, but so much improved that Claire considered it a major victory. And afterward Monkey followed him from the pen as calmly as Belle would have.

That accomplishment wrought a change for the better in Micah. He sat with Annie every night after dinner, and Claire saw the friendship between them blossoming into something more.

That Saturday, at the end of the third week of camp, Seth relieved Micah of his stable chores permanently and gave him the extra time to help Sonny. The other teens offered to give Micah some of their points, but Claire said no. He had already regained his hat and was well on the way to earning his boots. He needed to succeed on his own.

The last week of camp went quickly. Claire marveled at the changes four short weeks had wrought. The teenagers had bonded and now were the best of friends. Even Micah was eager to get back to school and start over. Claire knew there would be rough patches for him, and for Annie, too, but she was confident her camp had given them tools to help them cope and succeed.

Seth barely limped now. The physical activity of riding therapy, hiking and trail rides had hardened his muscles and honed his physique. Claire began to look forward to the end of camp, when she could have him to herself to discover all she didn't know about him.

There was a lot about falling in love that Claire was just discovering, too. That the sun shone brighter when Seth was near, that the misty mountains seemed more beautiful, that the breeze smelled sweeter, that laughter came easier and her frown could be erased by his smile. That his very appearance could stop her heart, quicken her breathing, make her body ache with eagerness to feel his slightest touch.

He had worked wonders with Micah, and she admired him for that. Micah had not mentioned his mother since he got to camp, and Claire delayed telling him about her circumstances until closer to the end of camp. But she'd learned that Mrs. Abbott would be in rehab through the end of summer, so she had to face the problem of what to do with Micah.

She updated Seth on the new development.

"I'm worried," she told him. "What's going to happen to him after camp is over? I hate to let him slip into the social services arena. It's so hard to get out again, and may destroy the confidence he's gained lately, little though that may be."

"Sonny told me the other day that Micah is good with mechanical work. Maybe he would take him on as a helper if Jon agrees."

"That would be wonderful!" Claire exclaimed. "Micah could live in the dorm until school starts."

"Maybe you could arrange to give the kid a small salary," Seth said. "It means a lot to a man to earn a wage for his work."

"I'll pay him myself, if I need to," Claire stated.

As soon as the arrangement was approved by Jon Rider, Claire told Micah.

"Are you kidding?" the boy said, with more enthusiasm than Claire had ever seen from him.

"If you want to do it and your mother gives permission, which I believe she will."

"I want to! Thanks so much, Claire."

"Actually, you should thank Seth. He came up with the idea and cleared it with Sonny."

Micah grew quiet.

"Something wrong?" Claire asked.

He shook his head. "No, just wondering why Seth would do that for me."

She smiled. "Because he's a good guy. And he wants to see you succeed as much as I do."

"Yeah, he *is* a good guy," Micah admitted. "He...you both gave me another chance when I didn't deserve it."

"What matters is how you use that chance."

• • • •

O N THE LAST SUNDAY of camp, Claire and Seth said goodbye to the kids as their parents picked them up. Annie cried on Claire's shoulder and promised to tell her mother what had happened to her. Mary Lou jokingly swore she intended to be bad at school so she could come back to camp next year. Always looking for responsible teens to help with her therapeutic riding program, Claire suggested she volunteer as an aide. Her mother readily agreed and promised Claire that Mary Lou would be at the stable in Little Lobo whenever she was needed. With newfound pride, Jason announced to his father that he could take care of a horse now and wasn't afraid of them anymore. Micah gave Annie a chaste kiss goodbye, but Claire suspected those two would be an item after school started.

When everyone had left except Micah, Seth and Claire, the three looked at one another as if for the first time. And in a way it was. Micah's new outlook was gratifying, even if he copped his old attitude now and then. Claire held hope that he would make graduation, and Seth was pushing him to apply to a tech school.

And she and Seth could be more open in their relationship, although with Micah in the bunkhouse, they still had to be discreet.

On Monday, Micah started working full days with Sonny, and Claire and Seth escaped for his scheduled therapy ride. She took the lead after the work was done but didn't head back toward the ranch.

"Where are we going?" Seth asked. "Not that I care, as long as you're leading. Nice view from back here."

"The view gets better a little higher up," Claire said with a teasing smile. "There's a line shack not far ahead. I'm thinking we might hunker down in there for a while."

"Works for me," Seth said.

They dismounted and urged the horses into the lean-to stable beside the cabin and went inside. The cabin was a rustic shack where cowhands could shelter from the elements or spend the night if they got caught out too late to get back to the ranch. A lantern sat on the table. One corner of the room had cabinets, and a camp stove on the counter. Narrow beds flanked two walls.

Claire's breath quickened as Seth's gaze ran the length of her body. His eyes turned dark and intense as he stared at her lips.

"Hard to believe we're actually alone, isn't it?" he said.

She reached for his hat, set it aside, then tousled his hair. The strands falling over his forehead gave him a sexy, devil-may-care look that sent shivers to her toes. He must have had a groupie following a mile long. And she probably didn't want to know how many of them had managed to seduce him over the years. No, she definitely did *not* want to know.

• • • •

S eth took her in his arms. Being with her every day the past few weeks had been heaven—and hell. He could hardly keep his hands off her, yet there was no way he could say and do what he wanted with the campers around all the time. Not to mention her father. And the Rider family. And the ranch hands.

There would be nobody to interrupt them here. They stood motionless, staring into each other's eyes, intoxicated by the heady isolation. Claire traced the scarred dimple in his cheek lightly with a fingertip, then moved her palms down his body, skimming over his shirt.

The wind whistled down the chimney and sunshine poured through the open door. The touch of her breath on his face sent a shudder of pure pleasure through him. Seth stared at the rough planked ceiling and wished they never had to go back.

"Do you know that I can't get enough of you? That every minute you're not in my arms is torture?"

"Oh, Seth, such a flatterer," she said. "You sure it's not just old ingrained habit?"

"Nope, this has nothing to do with habit. I don't how I'll get through the nights without you."

"I know the feeling."

He kissed her forehead. "Small lifetimes."

"Seth, we have so many decisions to make now."

"Let's wait until another day." He touched his lips to the tip of her nose. "Right now I'm not sure I could concentrate."

"Mmm, me neither." She closed her eyes and a smile played on her lips. "This is paradise."

"As close to heaven as I'll ever get," Seth agreed, his arms tightening and his mouth descending to send them on a long-awaited passionate journey.

Afterward, they lay in each other's arms as long as they could, until Seth glanced at his watch. "As much as I'd like to 'hunker down' longer, I think you have a lesson soon, don't you?" He told her the time.

"Oh, gosh, I do. Guess we have to get back."

"I'm going to remember where this shack is, though, in case we need to hunker down again. I could get used to this."

"Stop it, Seth!" she laughed, getting up to look for her clothes. "You're making fun of me."

"Far from it," he said with a broad grin. "I'm crazy about hunkering." He sat on the side of the bed and passed her clothes to her. "In fact," he said, "I vote for a little hunkering every day from now on."

• • • •

C LINT INVITED Claire and Seth to dinner a few nights later and mentioned that Rosie would be joining them. Sonny had taken Micah home to meet his family and have supper that evening.

When they arrived, they found Rosie and Clint gussied up in Sunday clothes. Her father had forgone a jacket but wore a bolo necktie as if it were a noose. Claire couldn't recall seeing her dad in a tie more than once before.

When Rosie and Clint weren't looking, Claire wiggled her finger back and forth, pointing at the two of them, and grinned at Seth. He gave a little nod, as if he was thinking the same thing—something was definitely afoot tonight.

She was glad now she had decided on a simple sundress rather than her usual jeans. Seth looked like a different man in a pale yellow dress shirt and creased khaki pants, with casual brown loafers. He'd left his hat off tonight and his light brown hair glistened, which made Claire want to run her fingers through it like she had earlier that afternoon in the shack. In fact, she wouldn't mind skipping dinner and taking him straight back to the shack now. She couldn't, however, so she helped Rosie serve a fabulous dinner of succulent roast beef, rosemary braised potatoes, fresh corn, squash and peas, with buttered homemade rolls.

Rosie's food deserved all their attention, but the four of them carried on a pleasant conversation while they ate. Afterward, Clint leaned back in his chair. "Looks I might be getting even fatter in the future," he stated, rubbing his belly.

"Oh?" Claire said.

"Yep. I asked Rosie to marry me last night, and for some crazy reason, she said yes. We wanted to share the news with you first."

"Crazy is right," Rosie said with her normal good humor. "But this old fellow needs somebody to take care of him."

"I agree with that," Claire said, rising to hug Rosie, then her father. "I'm so happy for you both!"

"You'll be in the wedding, won't you, Claire?" Rosie asked, glancing at Clint.

Claire sat down again. "Of course I will. I wouldn't miss it for anything. What's the date?"

"After summer is over," her dad said. "When there's a lull at the ranch."

"And before the holidays," Rosie added. "I have way too much to do then."

Rosie brought coffee, then she and Claire swapped ideas about the wedding ceremony and reception, which would be held at the ranch, while the men discussed football, livestock and ranching.

"I've been talking more to my brother about that bull-breeding operation," Seth told Clint. "He's pretty gung ho to get started. Guess we'll be looking for breeding stock soon."

"Where you planning on setting this operation?" the older man asked.

Claire was only half listening to Rosie now. Seth had talked a little about starting a business venture with his brother, but he hadn't gotten around to mentioning it would be breeding bulls. How had she envisioned their future together? Or had she tried to see it at all? She'd been so focused on camp.... And the past few days together had been too blissful to cloud with doubts.

She glanced Seth's way, then looked closer, noting the joy in his expression. His eyes shone, his face was eager, his speech animated. She realized only now that he hadn't shown such excitement in weeks—because he'd stopped talking about bull riding altogether after she'd told him about Cody. The fire in him had gone out, and she hadn't noticed until this conversation sparked it again.

"Lane has some property adjacent to my parents' ranch. He thought that might be best at first, until I can get a house built on my own land. Then we'd move it."

"So where is your land? Close to here?"

"Not far. A thousand acres, a few miles from Emigrant. I bought it last year with my earnings. I wanted something close enough to home that I could commandeer my brothers for help now and then."

He wasn't talking about riding now, just breeding, she assured herself. But Emigrant? Her riding school was in Little Lobo and Emigrant would be a much longer drive for her students living near Livingston and Bozeman. Did he expect her to relocate? With a rush of concern, Claire realized just how little she and Seth had talked about the future. What sort of compromise would it take to make a relationship work? But could she just walk away from him, as much as she'd come to love him?

"You know," said Clint. "Jon's got a couple of young bulls that buck pretty well. You might take a look at them. Could be a good start if you get the right cows."

"I'll talk to Lane about it."

Claire and Seth took their leave a short while later. Back at the bunkhouse, as they walked onto the porch, she said, "That's the first I've heard of a breeding farm."

Seth stopped. "You said you didn't want me bull riding because of your brother."

"That's one reason. But I wasn't kidding when I told you I don't like the mistreatment of animals."

Seth turned to her with his hands on his hips. "Claire, you just ate roast beef. You wear leather boots every day. Where's your argument?"

"It's different."

"Yeah, it's worse. Bucking bulls are worth thousands of dollars apiece. No contractor is going to let them be mistreated. They work eight seconds a night, max. I wouldn't mind that kind of—"

She cut him off. "I don't feel like arguing about this now. We'll talk about it tomorrow. I'm tired and I'm going to bed. Good night."

Claire stalked off, her heart pounding. A rush of anxiety swept through her, leaving her hands cold, her fingertips tingling. She didn't like this turn of events, but she was terrified to discuss it tonight, afraid of the outcome. Somewhere along the line, she'd fallen in love with Seth Morgan—or the man she thought he was. But maybe he wasn't that man at all. And maybe he'd conclude she wasn't worth all he'd have to give up.

• • • •

SETH STOOD ROOTED, watching Claire disappear into her room. What had just happened? He'd almost convinced himself he could live without riding bulls, if that's what it took to have Claire. Did she expect him to give up everything?

The light in her room went off almost immediately, but no way could Seth sleep. He sat down on the porch steps, brooding. There was no doubt in his mind that he loved Claire, but he wasn't sure he could live up to her expectations. He'd have no way to earn a living if he couldn't ride or ranch. Nothing to bring to her.

Deep in thought that led to no conclusions, he didn't realize she'd joined him on the porch until she sat down beside him. She was barefoot, wearing only lightweight pants and a T-shirt. She snuggled under his arm and he accommodated her, drawing her into his warmth.

"I'm sorry, Seth. You just took me by surprise."

"I should have mentioned it to you first. We've been so busy the past few weeks, seems like we never made time to talk about important things."

"But we have to now."

"Claire, darlin'," he said, easing her closer to cradle her in his arms, "you know I love you, don't you? You've made it pretty clear you don't want me to go back to bull riding, but what did you think I could do other than ranch?"

She wrapped her arms around him and gave him a soft kiss. "I honestly don't know. I guess I just pictured the white picket fence without the ranch house and bulls in the pasture."

"Well, here's the problem. You know I don't have a college degree. I'm not a 'dumb son-of-a-gun' like my father called me for throwing away that opportunity, but I'm beginning to think he had a small point about college or some sort of job training. Because frankly, Claire, I don't know how to do anything but ranch and ride bulls. I'm probably cut out of the will, too, so don't look for an inheritance."

"So you're thinking we might starve?" Claire said lightly.

Seth cuddled her closer. "No, I won't let us starve. I just don't know how I'll feed us at this point other than digging ditches."

The night grew colder and the moon rose to its full height, then began to drop behind the mountains as they held each other and stared at the inky sky studded with stars, which held no answers.

Eventually, they heard the sound of tires crunching on the gravel drive. The two of them separated quickly and slipped into their respective rooms before Sonny dropped Micah off at the bunkhouse.

• • • •

WITH CAMP OVER, Seth found himself at loose ends, with nothing much to do. Claire had resumed teaching a lesson at the ranch each morning and night, and he was left to his own devices. Except he had no challenges, no responsibilities other than working out hard in the mornings to get back into riding condition now that his leg was almost healed.

He didn't even have Micah to supervise. The kid had taken to mechanics like a duck to water and talked constantly of applying to the nearby tech school after he graduated. Seth saw the conflict in Micah, too. He loved living at the ranch, working for Sonny, but Annie lived in town and Micah was anxious to see her again.

Even knowing that his mother would be out of rehab soon and they would be living in the small rental house in town, Micah worried that she would revert to drugs again if things got rocky. Claire assured him that there would be follow-up visits and a support group to help her adjust.

For a while Seth considered the free time a vacation. He rode Rube into the mountains, fished, hiked until his leg was strong and pain-free. Then he grew bored and hired on as a hand at the Rider ranch rather than move back in with Libby. Since her father was readying his house to welcome his new bride, Claire remained in the dorm, along with Seth and Micah. Rosie often cooked for them, and when she didn't Claire whipped up something for the three of them in her father's kitchen. Seth liked having her so close, even though they still kept their separate quarters.

He was working up the courage to formally propose to Claire, hoping that would give his life some direction again. Her father had teased her one night about a double wedding with him and Rosie, which was fine with Seth. Of course, the date they'd chosen coincided with the Professional Bull Riders World Finals in Vegas, but as he reminded himself again and again, it didn't matter. He wouldn't be there.

Clint must have sensed his restlessness, because he increased Seth's responsibilities until he was busy from dawn to dusk. Coming home one afternoon from a long day of mending fences, Seth noticed a commotion around one of the corrals. Curious, he reined Rube over.

Inside the paddock a bucking bronc threw a cowboy high into the air. The rider landed with a thud, among the cheers and jeers of the spectators.

Several more horses and a number of bulls milled around in separate holding pens on the other side of the dusty, makeshift arena. Micah waved from his perch on the top rail of the fence on the other side of the corral and Seth acknowledged him with a nod. He watched a couple more bronc rides, his arms crossed lazily on the saddle horn. There must be a rodeo coming up nearby for them to be practicing, he figured.

Seth straightened and started to ride away, frustrated that he couldn't join in the excitement. Chance Shelton caught sight of him.

"Hey! Put a bull in the chutes!" Chance yelled. "There's a famous bull rider among us."

Seth stiffened. Chance had never beaten him in an event, and he wondered if that might be why the guy always gave him a hard time. The heckling on the day Seth had ridden with Natalie still rankled.

All eyes turned toward him and Rube now.

"Put that bull in there and flank him," Chance ordered loudly, pointing to a big yellow animal. "Come on, Seth. We got your bull ready. He looks a lot like Rotten."

Seth tipped the brim of his hat down and shook his head. "You boys have your fun without me." He nudged Rube, but a cowboy stepped off the fence and blocked his way. Deliberately, Seth thought.

"Come on, Seth, show us how," Chance taunted. "None of us here is as good as you."

Micah gazed at him expectantly. The bull snorted and pawed in the chute—a clarion call to Seth. His muscles tensed and his blood pounded in fervid anticipation of matching wits with an animal that outweighed him ten times over.

"Come on, Seth. Eight seconds. I'll time you." Chance crossed the arena, goading him.

Sweat popped out on Seth's upper lip. His mouth went as dry as a riverbed in winter.

God, how he wanted to get on that bull! He knew the feel of the animal quivering beneath him, imagined the rope tightening around his gloved hand. *Take a breath, nod for the gate. Explode into the arena. Eight seconds.* Surely Claire wouldn't begrudge him eight seconds. To prove to himself he could still do it. To shut up these hecklers who didn't think he could.

Claire—or that big golden bull across the way that looked like Rotten?

A promise made—or an overpowering need fulfilled?

A lifetime—or eight seconds?

Seth's chest heaved as his gaze shot from one face to the next of the men gathered around him. Men wondering why he didn't take the challenge. Wondering why he hesitated. Wondering if he was afraid of that bull.

Claire or...

Seth swallowed hard, reined Rube around and headed for the barn. Away from the jibes and jeers. Away from the disappointment he thought he saw in Micah's eyes. Away from it all, where he could sort out his priorities.

Claire or bull riding.

Which would it be? Because he knew he couldn't have both—but living without either one was going to be pure hell.

Quickly he dismounted and unsaddled Rube, slapping the roan on the rump to send him out to pasture with the other horses. Seth headed for his room to pack. He was glad to see Claire was busy with a lesson. He'd be gone before she finished. Maybe he'd call her tomorrow or the next day. If he didn't, she'd figure it out in time. Or maybe he'd figure himself out and come back. At the moment he was too rattled to think straight.

"Seth!" Micah stood in the doorway leading from Seth's room to the porch. "Where are you going?"

"I'm leaving for a while."

The teen stared at him. "Leaving? Why? Because of what happened out there?"

"No, not just that. It's something that's been building."

"You don't have to prove anything to those idiots. You told me I had to make good decisions. Well, don't *you?*"

"I'm making the best decision for everybody." Seth zipped the bag, hoisted it over his shoulder and grabbed his spare boots from beside the door. He brushed past Micah and headed for his truck. Micah caught up as he dumped the bag and boots into the backseat. When Seth climbed into the cab, Micah grabbed the door and wouldn't let him close it.

"Are you running out on Claire, too?"

Seth stared through the windshield at the long road ahead.

"Micah, you and Claire will be fine. And maybe I'll be back tomorrow. I don't know. I flat-out don't know."

Micah stepped away when he slammed the door. Seth backed out of the parking area and took off just as Clint strode up, with Claire right behind him.

Seth couldn't bear to look at her in the rearview mirror, standing there dumbstruck. He was glad when the dust swirled around his truck and blocked his view.

CHAPTER EIGHTEEN

SETH'S TRUCK DISAPPEARED in a cloud of dust. By the time he was out of sight, he must have been doing ninety.

"Where's he going?" Claire asked Micah.

He quickly explained to her and Clint what had happened at the corral.

"That son of a bitch Chance," Clint swore.

Suddenly Claire was jerked back to the past, standing in the middle of a rodeo parking lot, watching her brother's taillights disappear. Then he was gone—and she'd never seen him again.

Her hand flew to her mouth. "Cody! Seth! Oh, Seth, come back!"

"Claire?" her father said with concern.

She whirled away from him and ran to the bunkhouse for her keys and cell phone. Coming out, fumbling with the keys as she sped to her truck, she was pulled up short by Clint.

"Let me go!" she cried, unable to quell the hysteria rising in her like a storm surge. "I've got to catch him."

"Not like this, you don't."

"Don't you see? It's like Cody. I've got to stop him. Let me go, Daddy. I've got to get to him in time."

"Claire, child, calm down. You're not going anywhere this upset." Her dad pulled her around to face him.

"Seth's going to kill himself driving like that." She tried to break her father's grip. "Like Cody did. Just like Cody." Claire clawed at Clint's hands, desperate to escape. Her voice broke. "Don't you understand? You let Cody go and he died. I'm not willing to lose Seth that way!"

Clint gave her a gentle shake. "Claire! Listen to me. You've got to clear your own head before you take him on. He's not running from what happened here today. He's running from what you want him to be."

Claire shook her head in confusion. "No...he..."

"You can't try to make a man like Seth into something he's not. If you can't love him for who he is, then let him go." Clint released her, but Claire couldn't move as his words sank deep into her heart.

Claire fought back stinging tears as realization dawned. "I tried to do the same thing to Seth that you did to Cody, didn't I? I made him choose between two things he loved most. He was trying, wasn't he, Dad?"

Clint hugged her against him. "He was trying hard. You've got to give him the freedom to make his own choice, and then you have to decide if you can love him."

"I've got to talk to him, Dad." Claire climbed into her truck.

"Move over and give me the keys," he said. "I'll drive. You call him and tell him to pull over."

Clint turned to Micah. "Find Jon and tell him what happened. I'll be back as soon as I can."

Micah sprinted in the direction of the barns.

Claire grabbed a couple of fast-food napkins from the dashboard to scrub the tears from her eyes so she could see the numbers on the cell phone.

"Fasten your seat belt," Clint ordered as he whipped the truck backward, then shot forward down the dirt road.

Claire snapped the belt into place and punched in Seth's number, her fingers trembling. After several rings, her call went to his voice mail. She ground her teeth and tried once more. Voice mail again.

"He's not answering, Dad. What if something's happened to him already?"

"It hasn't. Maybe he's got the phone turned off."

"No, it's ringing, but he doesn't answer."

"Keep trying." Clint stopped briefly at the end of the ranch drive and turned onto the highway toward Little Lobo.

Claire dialed again and prayed to hear Seth's voice. She glanced at her father, who was concentrating on the road as they sped along.

She kept trying and still got no answer.

"Drive faster, Dad, please!"

Clint clenched the wheel and shook his head. "I'm goin' fast enough. No need in all of us being scattered along the roadside."

"He's not answering." Claire's heart seized as she thought about Cody again. "Something bad's happened. I know it has."

• • • •

S ETH HEARD HIS CELL PHONE ring again—the special ring he'd put in for Claire. He couldn't answer it. Not yet. He had his eyes locked on the road whipping under his truck and he was running as fast as he could.

His tire caught a pothole. The truck lurched, lost traction, skidded several yards before he regained control. His heart thundered as he realized how close he'd come to flipping out across a field.

Make a bad decision and suffer the consequences. And make others suffer, too. Wasn't that what he kept telling Micah? Claire had already lost a brother. She didn't deserve to have her heart broken again.

A fleeting glance at the speedometer told Seth he was going close to a hundred, and he could barely see the road anymore for the moisture filling his eyes. He braked until he could pull off onto a dirt side road that led to a pasture. He shut the truck down and just sat there, head cradled in his arms on the steering wheel.

His phone rang again. Had to be the tenth time she'd called. No doubt he'd scared her to death, taking off like that. An image of her beautiful hazel eyes filled with tears caused his own vision to dim again. He loved her more than life itself—and he wanted her to stop calling him, because he didn't know what to tell her.

The real problem, he was slowly realizing as he sat on this lonely side road with his head in his hands, was that he wasn't sure who he was anymore. And until he got that straightened out, he had no right to claim Claire's love.

Seth knew he could ride any bull out there, if his leg could stand up to the stress. The more important decision was whether he really *wanted* to keep riding, knowing that Claire would be terrified every time he straddled a bull.

This time when the phone rang, he reached to answer it, but it stopped abruptly. He was considering calling her back when the crunch of tires caught his attention. He looked into the rearview mirror, to find Claire's truck stopping right behind him. Had she been driving like a bat out of hell all the time she was calling? Trying to catch him? He should have answered her. She could have been killed!

Seth was out of the truck in a bound, upset for a totally different reason now. He breathed a sigh of relief when Claire exited on the passenger side and raced toward him with her arms outstretched.

"Damn good thing you weren't driving," he said gruffly.

"Why did you tear off like that?" she said furiously. "You could have killed yourself."

Clint gave him a scathing look as he climbed from behind the wheel. "And if I hadn't stopped Claire, you mighta got her killed, too. I don't want to see another stunt like that outta you."

The realization of what could have happened to Claire made Seth's muscles weak. He wrapped his arms around her, nodding to Clint over her shoulder. "Yes, sir, I understand."

"And look, Claire," her father said, "it ain't so bad if he's got a little cowboy in him...like me."

"I know." She nestled closer. "I want to stay and talk to Seth awhile, Dad. Will you drive my truck home?"

Clint pointed a finger at him. "Don't you drive over fifty bringing her back."

"Got it," Seth said.

When the Clint left, Seth lowered the tailgate of the truck, and they sat side by side. He hugged her close and kissed her, wanting to prolong every moment with her.... Yet he knew the foundation of their future was still shaky.

"So what now, Claire?"

"Start over?"

He shook his head slightly. "I can't be the man you want me to be. I tried to fit that mold, but today...today I..." He rested his chin on the top of her head. "I watched those cowboys in the corral and I wanted to get on that bull so bad I could taste it."

"And you didn't because of me."

Seth laughed softly. "I wish I could say that honestly. I didn't because I knew my leg wouldn't take it yet. But what worried me was not knowing what I would do if the doctor releases me to ride again."

"It was easier when you thought you didn't have a choice."

"Yep, easy to make promises, easy to let you think I could become somebody I'm not."

"Dad said I was doing the same thing to you that he did to Cody. Destroying your spirit."

"I guess in our own different ways that could be true. But I'm not Cody. I love what I do. And I'm *good* at it. It's who I am. And I...I don't know if I'd ever be satisfied going out injured."

He pulled her onto his lap and she wrapped her arms around his neck. "I love you so much, Claire. But I'm afraid I can't make you happy. I finally had to face the truth today—I'm not who you want me to be. The one thing I do well scares you to death."

"Losing you is what scares me." Claire couldn't keep the tremor from her voice. "Losing you either way."

She pushed his hair back off his face. "I learned more during camp than our campers did. I learned what kind of man you are. And I love that man. That's all there is to it. I love you."

"But can you love a bull rider?" Seth asked.

Claire's eyes were moist when she gazed at him. "With all my heart. I don't care what you decide about the future, as long as I'm a part of it."

"Even if I decide to go back full-time?"

"Even then. I love you, Seth, and I'll learn to live with it. Just don't expect me to watch you." She smiled then. "There's something else you should know," she said, snuggling closer. "I couldn't have hired a better counselor than you."

He searched her face and saw the truth there. Her words were a balm to his wounded soul, and his heart sang as the nightmare of the past few months faded, replaced by the bright hope of a life with Claire.

He hugged her tight, no words necessary. He might ride again, if the doc said he could—or he might choose not to. He and Claire would make that decision together when the time came. But one thing he knew for sure. Riding another bull wouldn't be what made him whole—it would be Claire's love.

EPILOGUE

TWO MONTHS LATER...

SETH WAITED BEHIND THE chutes. In the go-round last night, he'd been the first to ride, a sure indicator of how far he'd fallen in the standings while he was gone. The lowest-ranking rider rode first, the highest-ranking one last. But he'd covered his bull the full eight seconds to earn a decent score, and tonight, for the second go-round, he was in the middle of the pack.

Still, it felt great to be back. That old confidence filled him, made him cocky for the first time since his injury. None of his sponsors had dropped him, and his crisp white shirt and black protective vest were still plastered with big-name endorsement logos.

He grinned at the brand-new, hand-tooled leather chaps covering his legs, an unexpected gift that had arrived just this morning—from his father. Seth had never been as proud of a pair of chaps in his life.

His entire family sat in the stands, along with Clint, Rosie and the Riders. Even Natalie, Ben and the summer campers were up there somewhere. All waiting to watch his comeback. All but the one who mattered most. And that was the lone downer today. What he loved to do most frightened Claire so badly she couldn't watch.

He pressed his black Resistol hat low over his eyes, then looped his bull rope on the top rail of one of the gates, flexing and rosining it before he rode. He and Lane were putting together a business plan to start a breeding program. If Seth won enough money tonight, he would buy their first bucking bull. From their calculations, they figured Seth could retire in about four years, if he continued to earn what he had before the injury. Hopefully, Claire could stand the tension that long. If not, Seth knew he'd hang up his rope sooner, and he and Lane would simply build the business more slowly.

A shout went up from one end of the bleachers. A crowd of fans hung over the rail, shrieking for Seth's attention. He grinned and tipped his hat to Annie, Mary Lou and the Rider girls, eliciting gales of delight. One of the bullfighters who'd saved his life stopped and clapped him on the back. "Welcome home, Seth."

Home. This rarified world of testosterone and adrenaline and sheer animal power *was* his home. One of them, anyway. Going back to his parents' ranch had been one of the hardest things Seth had ever done. Gaining his father's forgiveness hadn't been as bad as he'd expected because Judd Morgan wanted his son back as much as Seth wanted a father again. They might never be as close as they'd been when Seth was a child, but they were forging a new bond that he hoped would last the rest of their lives. And his whole family loved Claire.

A few minutes later, a standing ovation rocked the stadium when the announcer called Seth's name. Then the chute opened and he exploded into the arena on his first bull of the night. He rode like the pro he was, in control, perfectly balanced on the back of the writhing, snorting mass of muscle, feeling no indication that he'd been laid up for months.

His high score put him first in the short-go, the final round of competition that would take place after intermission, which meant he would ride last. Back on top. Right where he loved to be. Where he belonged.

The announcer's gravelly voice came over the PA system, calling out the random matchups for the short-go. A hush fell over the crowd when the names of the final pair rang out.

Seth Morgan riding Rotten.

Behind the chutes, Seth grimaced and closed his eyes in disbelief. Not *Rotten!* Of the fifteen bulls in the pen, the luck of the draw had pitted him against his worst enemy.

"You owe me one, Rotten," Seth whispered.

What he remembered of that fateful ride seven months ago played through his mind like a broken record. The buzzer. The bull lurching to his knees. The pain. The months of recovery and wondering if he'd ever be here again. And now this.

As the other riders went before him, Seth kept to himself, trying to stay loose, to psyche himself up to get on that bull. Two animals left ahead of him. Decision time. He could walk away and leave it all behind—but if he chickened out now, he could never face these people again.

Forcing doubt out of his mind, he straddled Rotten fifteen minutes later—and could swear the big bull recognized him when he turned a red eye Seth's way, the challenge clear. Concentrating on staying focused, Seth went through the familiar motion of wrapping the bull rope around his hand. In spite of the risk, he used the suicide wrap today, pulling the last turn of rope between his ring finger and pinkie. Harder to release, it was the same wrap he'd used on Rotten before, when he couldn't get his hand out in time.

The flank man tightened the flank strap and Seth felt Rotten begin to quiver beneath him. Or was it Seth himself trembling? Didn't matter. A last deep breath. He nodded. The gate flew open.

Rotten blew out of the chute and whirled away from Seth's hand. Seth slipped an inch. Rotten felt it and surged forward. The screams of the crowd had never penetrated Seth's concentration before. But tonight, above the sound of Rotten's hooves thundering into the turf, the bull's wild snorts and the rush of blood in his own ears, Seth heard Micah yelling for him to hang on.

Determined not to disappoint the kid, Seth strained to adjust his seat. He tucked his chin and regained his balance and rhythm.

Six. Seven. Eight! The buzzer blared.

Seth yanked the end of the bull rope. In a flash of déjà vu, he found his hand stuck in the suicide wrap. Rotten bellowed and swung his head hard. Expecting to feel the bull coming down on him again, Seth gave the end of the rope a mighty tug. His hand came free. Rotten bucked high into the air and sent Seth flying. But he landed on his feet, stumbled a few steps and caught his balance. The crowd went wild. Seth raced to the fence and scrambled to the top to escape the marauding bull now trying to take out anybody or anything left in the arena.

In the stands a few rows up, Micah jumped up and down, cheering for him and hugging the person next to him.

"Hey, kid!" Seth slung his Resistol to Micah and yelled, "It's all yours. Let's see what you can do with it."

Grinning from ear to ear, Micah stepped aside to catch the hat, then tipped it down over his eyes the way Seth wore it.

And there beside him, the person he'd been hugging, was Claire. She was crying, but Seth got the feeling they might be happy tears this time.

He held out a hand toward her, beckoning her to him. She tried to get down the aisle, now blocked with people leaving or coming to the rail. Seth lost sight of her as fans and fellow riders gathered around to congratulate him. But he clung to the fence a few seconds longer, hoping to see her again. Then Micah broke through the crowd, clearing a path for Annie and Mary Lou.

And Claire.

"I already filled out my application!" Micah shouted above the din of the crowd. "I'm going to tech school, Seth. I'm going to learn to be a car mechanic like Sonny!"

"That's great!" Seth said. "I know you can do it."

His attention riveted on Claire. He caught her hand when she got close enough and pulled her to the rail to give her a gritty kiss. She didn't seem to mind.

"You're trembling," he said. "It's over. I'm okay."

"I know, but watching you ride Rotten again scared me to death. I can't believe I managed to stay for the whole thing." She took his face in her hands to kiss him again, then smiled. "But I have to admit, you looked real good out there."

A crush of fans surrounded them, trying to get to Seth. He pulled Claire near so that he could make his words heard. "I love you."

All she could do was nod vigorously as a bevy of young girls intruded, trying to touch him, vying for his attention.

Claire leaned over the rail, her mouth close to his ear. "I definitely need to get you married—as soon as possible."

When she would have moved back, Seth wrapped one arm around her waist and kept her next to him, while he scribbled autographs with the other hand.

Then Seth heard his name called over the PA system. His score of 92.5 had won the event. He pulled Claire to him and kissed her again.

"Wait right here while I get my money."

He suffered through the ceremony in the arena, made a short acceptance speech and shook hands with the man who handed him the first-place check. The arena was clearing, so he didn't have any trouble finding Claire and their families afterward.

He bounded up to the railing and over the top, grinning at Lane and their father, then took Claire in his arms. "That should pay for the honeymoon," he said.

Claire's eyes widened when she read the amount on the check. She looked at him in amazement, then smiled. "Or maybe it'll buy our first bucking bull."

Seth drew her into a long, passionate kiss in front of everybody. He was on top of the world, and his triumph over Rotten wasn't the only reason. The real victory was winning Claire's heart.

Life couldn't be any better.

ACKNOWLEGMENTS
Special thanks to the following for their help with researching this book.
If I got something wrong—blame me, not them!
Many thanks to:
D. J. Domangue, Professional Bull Rider who sustained an injury similar to Seth's and who graciously shared the experience in detail. Darren Epstein, Executive Director, Express Sports Agency, for introducing me to D.J. To Chris Shivers and Mike White, Professional Bull Riders, for introducing me to Darren.
Dr. Tandy Freeman, Sports Injuries, Dallas Orthopedic Center, surgeon extraordinaire to the Pro Bull Riders, for his information on leg injuries; to his assistant Val Worthington for shuffling my questions and his answers back and forth.
To Josh Peter, author of *Fried Twinkies, Buckle Bunnies, & Bull Riders: A Year Inside the Professional Bull Riders Tour* for putting me in touch with Dr. Tandy.
To Dale Butterwick, MSc, University of Calgary Sport Medicine Centre, for describing rodeo injuries and rehab. To Daniel Brister, steer wrestler, for general rodeo information.
To Carol Vallee, Meadowview Stables, Baton Rouge, for allowing me to observe her therapeutic riding classes, and to Priscilla Marden, CEFIP-ED, Horse Warriors, Jackson Hole, Wyoming for more information on equine-assisted therapy.

About Elaine

• • • •

From an early age, Elaine wanted to write stories.

Her first short story was published in her small town newspaper when she was in third grade.

Her first novel, *Roses for Chloe*, a Berkley-Jove Haunting Hearts release in 1998 was an RWA RITA Contest finalist. Her next three books were Harlequin Superromance® novels, one of which, *Make Believe Mom*, also went on to become a RITA finalist. Later, Elaine took a leap of faith into indie publishing with her romantic thriller *The Caverns*, the first book in the Tennessee Mountain Home series.

After moving back home to Alabama, Elaine enjoys reconnecting with family and high school friends and visiting her son, daughter-in-law and grands in New York. She lives with her rescue dog Mariah who loves nothing more than chasing squirrels and snakes through the woods.

Elaine's Books

Little Lobo Series – *Heartwarming stories set in the mountains of Montana*
Make-Believe Mom – Book 1
Accidental Dad – Book 2
Along For the Ride – Book 3

Roses For Chloe – *A Louisiana Ghost Story*

The Caverns – *A Romantic Thriller set in the Smoky Mountains of Tennessee*